MRS PARGETER'S PRINCIPLE

A Selection of Recent Titles by Simon Brett

The Charles Paris Theatrical Series

A RECONSTRUCTED CORPSE
SICKEN AND SO DIE
DEAD ROOM FARCE
A DECENT INTERVAL *
THE CINDERELLA KILLER *

The Fethering Mysteries

BONES UNDER THE BEACH HUT
GUNS IN THE GALLERY *
THE CORPSE ON THE COURT *
THE STRANGLING ON THE STAGE *
THE TOMB IN TURKEY *

The Mrs Pargeter Mysteries

MRS PARGETER'S PACKAGE
MRS PARGETER'S POUND OF FLESH
MRS PARGETER'S PLOT
MRS PARGETER'S POINT OF HONOUR
MRS PARGETER'S PRINCIPLE *

* *available from Severn House*

This first world edition published 2015
in Great Britain and the USA by
Crème de la Crime, an imprint of
SEVERN HOUSE PUBLISHERS LTD of
19 Cedar Road, Sutton, Surrey, England, SM2 5DA.
Trade paperback edition first published
in Great Britain and the USA 2015 by
SEVERN HOUSE PUBLISHERS LTD.

British Library Cataloguing in Publication Data

Brett, Simon author.
  Mrs Pargeter's principle.
  1. Pargeter, Mrs. (Fictitious character)–Fiction.
  2. Women detectives–Fiction. 3. Detective and mystery stories.
  I. Title
  823.9'2-dc23

ISBN-13: 978-1-78029-074-4 (cased)
ISBN-13: 978-1-78029-557-2 (trade paper)
ISBN-13: 978-1-78010-653-3 (e-book)

All Severn House titles are printed on acid-free paper.

Severn House Publishers support the Forest Stewardship Council™ [FSC™],
the leading international forest certification organisation. All our titles that
are printed on FSC certified paper carry the FSC logo.

Typeset by Palimpsest Book Production Ltd.,
Falkirk, Stirlingshire, Scotland.
Printed and bound in Great Britain by
TJ International, Padstow, Cornwall.

MRS PARGETER'S PRINCIPLE

A Mrs Pargeter Mystery

Simon Brett

CRÈME de la CRIME

To Liz and her mother,
persons of discrimination
(because they like my books)

And to Jenny Nagle who won in a charity auction
at Westonbirt School in aid of the
James Hopkins Trust
the right to have her name included in this book

ONE

G iven the fact that they were all at a funeral, it was a surprisingly jolly occasion. But then Sir Normington Winthrop had led a very happy and full life – considerably fuller, in fact, than many of the mourners in the Abbey knew.

Certainly fuller than his widow knew. It had been a second marriage for Normington, and Helena, the new Lady Winthrop, fearful of feeling jealous of his deceased first wife and for other reasons best known to herself, had enquired very little about her husband's past.

Which, in the view of a few people attending his funeral, was probably all to the good.

The congregation that April morning represented quite a wide spectrum of society. Cabinet ministers and City magnates filled the front few pews. Then there were representatives of the many charities to which Sir Normington had devoted so much of his money and time, as well as members of his livery companies. Business associates, many in the white robes of their Middle Eastern origins, occupied more pews. And any spaces left were filled with more of the Great and the Good.

But one row contained three people who looked different from the rest. Not out of place exactly, but different. The focus of the group, to whom the two men seemed to defer, was a comfortingly plump woman wearing a black dress with a design of bright-red poppies on it, which contrived to look both striking and respectful of the occasion. A black straw hat and some fairly elaborate jewellery added to the ensemble. And black high heels showed off surprisingly well-shaped legs.

On her right sat a good-looking young man in a dark chauffeur's uniform. To the other side of her was a tall, lugubrious man with the mournful expression of a bloodhound for whom the Botox hadn't worked. He was slightly scruffily dressed, but did have a black tie anchored round his crumpled shirt collar.

The expression on the face of each man, when looking at the woman, demonstrated a devotion little short of adoration.

The woman's name was Mrs Pargeter.

The chauffeur beside her was called Gary. He ran a very busy car-hire company, but he always saw to it that he was personally available when Mrs Pargeter required transport.

The tall man was a private detective called Truffler Mason. The one thing the two men had in common was that they had both worked for Mrs Pargeter's late husband. And she had found them entered into the most valuable bequest that her husband had left her – a little black book containing the names of all his associates with descriptions of their specialist abilities. It was amazing what services she could access through that little black book, where names and contacts were stored under such headings as 'Lock Specialists', 'Missing Persons Investigators' or 'Armourers'.

The little black book, indeed, provided the sole reason why Mrs Pargeter was attending the funeral. The name of Normington Winthrop appeared in its pages, and she thought the possibility unlikely that there were many Normington Winthrops around, so when she read the obituary and funeral notice in the *Daily Mail* Mrs Pargeter decided she had to attend. It was a matter of principle for her to show proper respect to anyone who had worked for her late husband. Besides, it was the kind of occasion where she might well meet other of the late Mr Pargeter's associates. And if she found any of them suffering any kind of hardship, Mrs Pargeter regarded it as another matter of principle to provide help for them. She was really just carrying on her husband's unfinished business.

And if either of the men sitting in the row with her had been asked what the late Mr Pargeter's business actually was, each one of them would unhesitatingly have replied that he was a philanthropist.

A fleet of limousines took the mourners from the Abbey to an exclusive hotel near Victoria Station (rumoured to be patronized by minor royals for saucy frolics), where in a private room the post-funeral drinks would be consumed.

Helena Winthrop, in designer black, did not look prostrated

by grief, but then she had been brought up in the upper-class British tradition that any display of emotion was unseemly and embarrassing. Also, her face no longer had the capacity for much change of emotion. Feeling the approach of age, she'd had some work done, which had left her with an expression of permanent surprise at how old she was.

She had acted as hostess at many public events for her husband and appeared to bring the same professionalism to this one as she had to all the others. The absence of Sir Normington on this occasion was not something to which she thought attention should be drawn . . . though her guests did seem to want to keep talking about him.

Mrs Pargeter, experienced in widowhood, wondered whether Helena Winthrop would fall apart into a weeping mess the minute she got back to her empty Mayfair home, but rather doubted it. Unshakeable stoicism was ingrained into women of Helena's class. She had spent so long suppressing her emotions, Mrs Pargeter reckoned, that she wouldn't recognize a genuine one if it bit her on the bum.

The men who had shared the row in the Abbey with Mrs Pargeter did not recognize anyone else at the reception, which she thought was a little odd. If Normington Winthrop had really worked with the late Mr Pargeter, she would have expected more of his former associates to come to the funeral. Mutual support had been one of the guiding principles of her late husband's business. She had an uncharacteristic moment of doubt. Maybe the world *did* contain more than one Normington Winthrop.

Though Mrs Pargeter was quite capable of introducing herself easily to strangers on such occasions, this time she was content to stay within her own group. She saw a lot of Gary when he chauffeured her around, but it was a while since she'd had a good chat with Truffler Mason. Anyway, the champagne and the nibbles were of a very high quality. And the waiting staff were very efficient at keeping everyone's glasses topped up. So it was not an unpleasant way of passing a Thursday morning.

Truffler was a close colleague who had worked on most of the late Mr Pargeter's projects. After his patron's death, like many of the great man's former employees, he had adapted his skills into a more traditionally legitimate area of endeavour. In Truffler's case this had meant setting himself up as a private investigator in the Mason De Vere Detective Agency. (There was, incidentally, no 'De Vere' involved in the business. Truffler just thought the extra name made his set-up sound classier. And it avoided time-wasting phone calls from men with funny handshakes who kept talking about lodges.)

'So, how's business?' asked Mrs Pargeter, in a voice that still retained a hint of her Essex origins.

'Can't complain,' said Truffler, in a voice that sounded as though it was permanently complaining. If he had been announcing that he'd won the jackpot on the National Lottery, he would still have sounded as though he'd just lost a close relative. It was just the way he talked.

'A bit of missing persons stuff,' he went on, 'but it's still mostly matrimonial. Wives checking on husbands, husbands checking on wives. You keep reading about "open marriages", people not getting upset about their partner having the odd fling . . . Well, you wouldn't believe it from the kind of work that comes my way. Betrayal still seems to hurt as much as it ever did. I'd say people are more vindictive now than they ever have been. Lot of them still insist that if there's evidence of an affair, then that's the end of the marriage.'

Mrs Pargeter smiled sympathetically. Fortunately, that was something she and her late husband had never had to worry about. They had both been so wrapped up in each other that the thought of sneaking off with someone else would never have occurred to either of them. She had, she knew, been very lucky. And though in her years of widowhood other men had come on to her – she was still a very attractive woman – she had never been even mildly tempted. She knew that none of them could ever match up to the late Mr Pargeter.

'But, of course,' said Truffler, 'you know that if ever you have need of my services, you have only to say the word, and I'll drop everything to help you out. You know that, don't you?'

'I do indeed. And it's a very comforting thing to know.' Mrs Pargeter smiled a warm broad smile. She was very appreciative of the nurturing backup she received from her late husband's associates. 'And anything on the Old Boy front?'

It was part of a code between them. The 'Old Boys' referred to the wider circle of people (mostly men) who had been involved in the late Mr Pargeter's business enterprises. Truffler Mason kept in touch with them, quick to detect if any were experiencing troubles in their lives. He acted as a kind of benign pension consultant (if that expression is not an oxymoron), reporting cases of hardship to Mrs Pargeter. And she would frequently provide financial aid to the needy from the very considerable fortune that her late husband had amassed during his hard-working life.

'Heard of a couple for whom things aren't so fine and dandy,' Truffler replied. 'Do you remember old "Gizmo" Gilbert?'

'I might have heard the name, but I never met him.' Mr Pargeter had, quite shrewdly, only introduced his wife to a very close circle of his associates. One of his mantras had always been 'what you don't know about you can't tell anyone else about'.

'Gizmo was one of the greats,' said Truffler Mason.

'I'll say,' Gary the chauffeur endorsed gleefully.

'Electronic whizz, old Gizmo,' Truffler went on. 'Way ahead of the game, he was. Now we take for granted remote controls on everything: change channel on your telly, turn your lights on, close your curtains. Gizmo Gilbert was doing that kind of technology way before it was available commercially.'

'Yes.' Gary chuckled. 'Remember that thing he done that could open the main doors of the Shoreditch branch of NatWest Bank from the other side of the road? And open the vaults and all?'

'I'll say!' For a moment Truffler Mason almost sounded enthusiastic. 'One invention of his that stays with me is the thing that jammed the firing mechanisms on all the guns Dobbyboy Pelton's lot was going to use in the Southampton bullion job.'

'And then there was that little zapper he invented what put an electric current through the handcuffs the cops were carrying . . .' Gary's words trickled away as he saw the expression of bemused puzzlement on Mrs Pargeter's face.

'I'm sorry,' she said with naive innocence, 'but I'm afraid I haven't understood a word of what you've just been saying.'

'Ah, well, it wasn't really that important,' mumbled Gary.

'No.' Truffler Mason also recovered himself. 'What *is* important, though, is that Gizmo Gilbert's fallen on hard times. He's still trying to produce his inventions . . .' He caught a look in Mrs Pargeter's eye which made him say, 'Different stuff now. More domestic applications than, er, professional. But nobody seems to want what he's offering any more. Modern technology's, like, caught up with him. Besides, he's nearly eighty, and the arthritis is getting to the old fingers. He's not, like, as dexterous as he used to be in his workshop.'

'So he needs help?' asked Mrs Pargeter.

'Certainly. But it's got to be done subtle, like.'

'How d'ya mean?' Gary asked.

'Well, a geezer like Gizmo Gilbert's got his pride. He won't take a handout from no one – even refuses to take his state pension. Says he didn't contribute enough in the right way to justify him having it. So the approach has got to be, like I say, subtle.'

'"Subtle" is my middle name,' said Mrs Pargeter.

'Really?' said Gary. 'That's unusual. Why did your parents choose that?'

She looked into his honest, confused face and decided it wasn't worth explaining. Instead, she said to Truffler, 'Give me Gizmo Gilbert's contacts and I'll pay him a visit. Anyone else in trouble?'

'Well, there's "Passport" Pinkerton. Know the name?'

Again, Mrs Pargeter replied vaguely that she might have heard it mentioned. 'Why, what's wrong with him?'

'I'm afraid he's snuffed it,' said Truffler Mason, at last finding a topic appropriate to his lugubrious delivery.

'I am sorry to hear that. Natural death, was it?'

'Yes. Pancreatic cancer.'

'Oh dear.'

'The thing is, though, I only found out recently, but since your husband died, Passport Pinkerton never had two pennies to rub together.'

Instant concern came into Mrs Pargeter's violet-blue eyes. 'We should have helped him.'

'He didn't make it easy for us to do that. Moved to the Costa Brava and lived undercover there, different name and all.'

'But what went wrong with his career? My husband was always very good at helping people out with vocational retraining and what-have-you.'

'Yes, he was. Very generous man.' Truffler allowed a moment of silent respect. 'Passport's problem was – like Gizmo Gilbert's, though in a different way – the new technology. I mean, he was an artist, old Passport. Learnt his skills when he was a prisoner of war in Colditz. He could reproduce any document you wanted – all done with his ink-pens and paint brushes. And he still made a good living from that after the war.

'But then all this fancy new printing and photocopying technology come in. No need for the gifted artist then; just someone who could feed data into a computer. And another fine traditional craft had been superseded.' Truffler Mason shook his head at the inexorable – and not always beneficial – advance of science.

'Why did Passport Pinkerton change his name when he went out to Spain?' asked Mrs Pargeter.

'Well . . .' Truffler phrased his words carefully. 'I think he may have done some things that put him on the wrong side of the law.'

Mrs Pargeter tutted. 'And my husband was always so insistent that his associates should stay on the right side of the law.'

'I know. In Passport's case, though, I think it was incompetence rather than criminality that let him down.'

'Yes.' Gary grimaced. 'Putting his contact details in the *Yellow Pages* under "Forgery" didn't help.'

Truffler Mason nodded morose agreement.

'Hm.' Mrs Pargeter nodded too. 'So, what's needed? Money to pay the funeral expenses?'

'I think that might be handy – unless it's already happened. But more importantly, Passport's got this daughter called Samantha, and I gather she's feeling the pinch.'

'Introduce me to her,' said Mrs Pargeter.

A man whose shoulders were so broad that he'd have looked better in a T-shirt than in the dark suit he was wearing approached their little group. Without preamble he addressed the one female member. His public school-educated voice was at odds with his bruiser-like appearance. 'I'm told you're the widow of the late Mr Pargeter.'

She didn't deny it.

'I just want to say I don't want you talking to Lady Winthrop.'

'I think whether I do that or not,' said Mrs Pargeter evenly, 'is rather up to me.'

'But there's nothing for you to say to her.'

'I believe it is appropriate at such occasions to offer condolences to the bereaved.' As well as formality, there was a new iciness in her tone.

'Not in this case,' the man almost snarled. 'Keep away from her.'

There was a restlessness in the two men either side of Mrs Pargeter, both of whom reckoned the correct response to the man's manner was a firm fist to the chin. Gary the chauffeur was already clenching his hand in preparation. But Mrs Pargeter calmed them with a gesture.

'Anyway,' the man went on, 'it is not appropriate for you to speak to Lady Winthrop. You haven't been introduced to her.'

'If you're a stickler for that convention,' said Mrs Pargeter, 'then why haven't you introduced yourself to me?'

He was a little thrown by that and conceded his name. 'I'm Edmund Grainger.'

'Well, Edmund Grainger, I don't really see why I should do what you tell me.'

'Because if you don't –' his voice hissed with menace – 'it'll be the worse for you.'

At that threat, Truffler Mason also clenched his fists. But again she defused the tension with a gesture.

'We're leaving now,' she said with considerable dignity. 'I have never liked to stay in a place where I am not wanted.'

And she was still dignified as she led Gary and Truffler out of the room.

TWO

I t was on the Friday afternoon that Mrs Pargeter went to visit Gizmo Gilbert. The voice that answered her morning call had been ancient but very precise and, when he heard the identity of his caller, suitably delighted. 'My dear Mrs Pargeter, it would be a huge pleasure to meet you. When I think of all your late husband did for me . . .' It was a litany which she had heard often, but of which she never tired. 'So if there is anything I can do for you, Mrs Pargeter – anything at all – you have only to say the word.'

She did not think it appropriate to say that her visit concerned more what *she* could do for him. At least metaphorically, 'Subtle' remained her middle name.

The house stood out in a terrace not far from the many amateur football pitches of the Hackney Marshes. Stood out because it was the only one in the street yet to undergo 'gentrification'. It alone still had the windows which had been put in when it was originally built (in the early Edwardian period). It alone had no coach lamps, pastel paintwork, window-boxes or designer brass knockers. Its shabbiness was defiant, and Mrs Pargeter anticipated that this defiance might be a characteristic of the house-owner she was about to meet.

She hadn't wanted to arrive in the Bentley, so Gary had driven her there in a much less ostentatious Skoda Octavia. Even then she'd insisted that he let her out around the corner so that to Gizmo Gilbert she would appear to have arrived on foot.

The paint on the cracked front door had been white once, but was now flaking and in places worn away completely. The knocker was ancient and tarnished, but it resounded unexpectedly loudly when raised and dropped.

Gizmo Gilbert looked as though his body had been slowly eroded – as if he'd started out with normal human dimensions, which had been whittled away until now no cushion of flesh remained between his bones and their covering of parchment-like skin. The grey suit with dark stripes that he wore was floppy with age. Many new holes had been punched into his black belt to still give it some purchase on his narrow hips. The thin striped tie had ruched up the overlarge collar of his white shirt when he'd tightened it around his scrawny neck. His knuckles were swollen with arthritis.

'Mrs Pargeter!' he cried, his bony fingers clasping her plump ones. 'This is such a pleasure. I never thought I'd be so lucky as to meet you, but I've heard so much about you from your late husband.'

'He talked about me, did he?' she asked, caught in a moment of emotion.

'All the time. He swore that having you in his life made him the most fortunate creature on God's earth.'

'Oh,' she said, touched.

'But I can't keep you standing here on the doormat. Come in, come in. Now, I'm sure you'd like a cup of tea.'

'That would be very nice, thank you.'

The wallpaper in the hall Gizmo Gilbert led her through was shabby and worn in places, but everything in the house was spotlessly clean and there was an invigorating smell of furniture polish. He ushered her into a front parlour, the three-piece suite of which was a homage to the chintz of another era. On a tray on the small table stood a teapot encased in a silver-coloured orb with a round black ball on top, with two green Denby ware cups and saucers, matched by milk jug and sugar bowl. Rich tea biscuits were aligned on a green plate, and the tin in which they were kept was also on the tray. Its patriotic design commemorated the 1947 wedding of the future Queen Elizabeth II to Philip Mountbatten, the Duke of Edinburgh.

Having settled Mrs Pargeter in an armchair, Gizmo Gilbert poured tea for her with hardly a tremor in his skeletal hands. She accepted the proffered rich tea biscuit – and, indeed, obeyed his injunction to 'take two'.

When they were cosily settled, he asked again, as he had on the telephone, 'Now, Mrs Pargeter, what can I do for you?'

'Well . . .'

'Is it something related to your late husband's business?'

'I suppose it is in a way, yes.'

Gizmo Gilbert's faded eyes sparkled as he said, 'I have been waiting a long time for this call.'

'Oh?'

'I had heard rumours from other former, er . . . work colleagues that you was continuing your late husband's business, but only with your phone call this morning did I know that those rumours was true.'

Mrs Pargeter was very keen not to give a misleading impression. 'They're true to an extent, Gizmo . . . May I call you Gizmo?'

'Please do.'

'But I am not so much continuing my husband's business as completing his *unfinished* business.'

'Ah.' There was an unmistakable note of disappointment in the monosyllable. 'So you mean you're not undertaking *new* business of the kind that your husband conducted with such brilliance?'

'I fear not. I just don't think I share the unique skill-set that my husband possessed.'

'No, you're probably right there. I don't think anyone did. He was, in the literal sense of the word, unique.'

'Exactly.'

'Hm.' The old man wryly screwed up his thin lips. 'I can't deny a sense of sadness to hear you saying that the glory days will never be repeated. When I think of some of the work I did for your husband . . . particularly the gizmo I invented for the Shoreditch NatWest job . . . I get a feeling of—'

'I'm afraid,' Mrs Pargeter interposed gently but insistently, 'that my husband talked to me very little about the details of his work.'

'Ah. Ah well . . .' Gizmo Gilbert still sounded nostalgic for the days that would never come again. 'There's something wonderful about working with people whose skills you admire, and your husband was highly skilled in what I believe is now called "team-building". He got together the best experts in every area, all highly efficient specialists, and he nurtured their talents. That's why he was simply the best in the business.'

Mrs Pargeter smiled gratefully. She appreciated the tact with which Gizmo Gilbert avoided being more specific about her late husband's professional life.

'We were a great team,' the old man reminisced. 'Your husband was a brilliant picker of men. A good judge of character. He hardly ever got it wrong, and when he did it was all down to his trusting nature. Being a man of such outstanding honesty himself, he found it difficult to believe that everyone else was not like him.'

Mrs Pargeter was content to let this paean to her late husband continue. The old boy was clearly enjoying it, and she was under no time pressure to get on to the real purpose of her visit.

'Of course, one of the worst times he was betrayed – or very nearly betrayed – was in the case of "Magnet" Mitchell. Did you ever hear about that?'

Mrs Pargeter once again apologized, repeating that her husband had talked to her very little about his work.

'Well, he was called Magnet because things had a strange habit of getting stuck to his fingers. No, give him his due, he was a brilliant burglar.'

Mrs Pargeter frowned vaguely, as if she had never before heard that last word. But Gizmo Gilbert didn't notice her reaction and went on: 'One of the absolute best, he was. Old Magnet could break in anywhere. If that kind of job needed doing it was Magnet your old man always called on. Result was he knew all the inside workings of the business. Mr Pargeter trusted him with everything.

'But little did he know the serpent he was nursing in his bosom. Old Magnet was taking notes all the time, building up, like, a dossier on your husband's empire. Do you know what he turned out to be, after all?'

'No,' Mrs Pargeter replied with complete honesty.

'He was only an undercover cop, wasn't he?'

'Really?'

'Yeah. There was a pretty big bust-up in the team when that news came out, I can tell you. About what should be done to the traitor. Your husband, who was always a man of peace, I reckoned, didn't want to take any action. Well, not action of a violent kind, anyway. He even thought we could take advantage of Magnet's inside knowledge of the police force, use him like a kind of double agent, get him to give us advance warning of any raids the cops were planning, that kind of thing. But not everyone in the team agreed with your old man on that. There was some young hotheads around back then, who didn't share your husband's dislike of violence.

'Anyway, a few weeks after the discovery of who Magnet really was, he was killed in a crash on his motorbike. Thought to be an accident – indeed, I'm pretty sure the old coroner come up with a verdict of "accidental death" – but none of us really bought that. I don't think your husband did either. Maybe coincidence, but soon after that a couple of youngsters we worked with – people of the pro-violence persuasion – suddenly found themselves off Mr Pargeter's payroll. I'm still pretty sure the reason for that was they'd fixed Magnet's death.'

Gizmo Gilbert sighed. 'Happy days,' he said. 'Never been happier than when I worked for your old man. Ah well . . . At least I've still got my memories of him.'

'As have I,' Mrs Pargeter agreed mistily. Then, pulling herself together, she went on, 'But I gather from Truffler Mason—'

'Dear old Truffler. Yes, he still keeps in touch. Lovely geezer. Still always sounds like the sky's about to fall in on him.'

'I don't think that'll ever change.'

'No. I got money on the fact nobody'll ever see him laughing.' The old man chuckled.

'Anyway, Truffler told me you were being as inventive as ever. Still coming up with the gizmos, eh?'

'Yeah, I keep my hand in. But it's not the same. Too much competition. When your husband got me involved in using that remote-control technology it was new. Now every tinpot cat burglar reckons he's an IT expert.'

'Really?' said Mrs Pargeter blandly. 'I wouldn't know about that, love. But Truffler implied to me that you might now be concentrating on a different area of the business?'

'How d'you mean?'

'How did he put it? He said that you were working on inventions that had more of a . . . domestic than professional application.'

'Oh, right. Yes, I've tried. But it's tough. There's a lot of competition out there. Remote controls for things round the house, they're ten a penny. And very shoddily produced, may I say? Mostly in China. At least when I made something, it was durable. Looked pretty good and all.'

'A work of art?'

'Well, I'm not one to blow my own trumpet, but, though I say it myself, some of them *were* bloody works of art. Actually, Mrs Pargeter . . .' His voice took on a new intimacy. 'There's something I've been working on recently that could have been designed absolutely with you in mind.'

'Really?'

'It runs on batteries, and it's called "The Widow's Comforter".'

'Is it?' said Mrs Pargeter.

Gizmo Gilbert clearly felt more at ease in his workshop than he did in other areas of the house. The space, which appeared to take up most of the remaining ground floor, had been custom designed and was spotlessly clean. But it was not the clean-ness of somewhere unused. There was an air of ongoing projects about the place, of experiments not yet fully developed. And the neatness of a proud workman who regarded tidying up at the end of it as part of a day's work.

Round three walls of the space ran a continuous workbench, above which serried ranks of tools were slotted into their allotted places. Vices, adjustable magnifying glasses, highly focused lamps, lathes and a variety of other power tools were fixed to the bench at intervals.

Gizmo Gilbert said nothing as he led Mrs Pargeter across to a particular section of the work surface where a metal safe was affixed to the wall. Taking from his pocket a key ring adorned with a variety of small remote controls, he pressed a sequence of three and the safe door clicked open.

Inside, nestled in a purpose-built cut-out of charcoal-grey foam rubber, was a device made of lighter grey metal. About four inches long, it had the look of an oversized car fob. He slipped the gizmo out of its moulding and, cupping it in his spidery hand, held it across to Mrs Pargeter.

'This,' he said proudly, 'is "The Widow's Comforter".'

'Oh?' she asked cautiously. 'And what exactly does it do?'

'I address you, Mrs Pargeter,' he replied, 'with the greatest respect, but – I hope you will not mind my using the word – as a widow.'

'That is undeniably what I am. It may not be a role that I would have wished to take on, but yes, I am a widow.'

'And there are many occasions when a widow must regret the absence of her deceased spouse.'

'Undoubtedly that is true.'

'Particularly, I would imagine, at the end of the day as the widow prepares herself for her lonely bed.'

'Ye-es,' said Mrs Pargeter, not entirely certain where this was going.

'It is at such moments when that loss of a husband must be felt most keenly.'

She said nothing, waiting to see what came next.

'There are things that only a husband can do for his wife.'

A silence ensued.

'I refer particularly to the business of getting her clothes off.'

'Do you?'

'And this is where my invention will prove absolutely invaluable.'

'Oh?'

'Many women's dresses, I have observed over the years, Mrs Pargeter, are designed with a zip down the back.'

Mystified, she agreed.

Suddenly, Gizmo Gilbert opened another metal door on his wall to reveal, stretched downwards in a frame, a fully zipped-up zipper. 'Press the button on "The Widow's Comforter", Mrs Pargeter,' he ordered dramatically.

She did as instructed. Instantly, the zipper in the frame unzipped.

Cocky as a conjuror who has just rejoined the two parts of his saw-bisected lady, Gizmo Gilbert announced, 'And that is what "The Widow's Comforter" does. It works on every kind of zip so far invented. And solves for every widow the terrible problem of having no husband to unzip her dress at the end of the day!'

'It's brilliant,' said Mrs Pargeter with some relief.
The inventor smiled with gratification.
'Just one thing, though, Gizmo . . .'
'What's that?'
'I think you ought to change the name.'

Mrs Pargeter was still holding her host's latest invention when
they returned to his front room. She graciously refused his
offer to make more tea, feeling a warm glow because she had
suddenly seen a way of helping Gizmo financially without
threatening his proud independence. To achieve this she would
need to employ a service set up by another of her late husband's
former employees.

He wasn't really called Armitage Shanks, but (being a well-
known firm of sanitary wear manufacturers) it was a popular
joke name for any all-purpose actor, and so that was what his
associates called him. When legitimate theatre work was
unavailable (which, as for the majority of actors, was most of
the time), the late Mr Pargeter would often find little jobs for
Armitage Shanks to do. Jobs which took full advantage of his
thespian skills. It was amazing how often there would be an
opening in his business ventures for someone to play a loss
adjuster, a successful investor or the victim of some unspeak-
able scam.

Armitage Shanks had also done a very creditable line in
police officers calling from scenes of non-existent crimes.
In this way, on many occasions valuable police resources had
been conveniently diverted away from the venues where the
real crimes were taking place. The actor got far more satisfaction from these performances than he had from many of his
stage and television roles.

But after his patron's death, like so many of the late Mr
Pargeter's employees, Armitage Shanks diversified into less
hazardous areas and set up his very successful franchise –
SomeoneAtTheOtherEndOfTheLine.com. This was a service
which supplied exactly what it said on the tin: a real person
with whom the caller could conduct a rather less real conversation. Though the company name was for a website, almost
all of its actual business was conducted on the phone. An

initial approach would be made online, defining the exact service required, the agreed fee and the timing of the relevant call.

Hearing a genuine human voice on the line was somehow more reassuring for listeners than seeing any number of claims spelled out on the Internet. And *SomeoneAtTheOtherEndOfTheLine.com* supplied those genuine human voices. It also supplied a lot of welcome work for Armitage Shanks's many underemployed actor friends.

The applications for its services were infinite, both at the professional and at the personal level. In negotiations for the purchase of a car or a house, it was frequently useful for the seller to be able to talk on the telephone to someone who had made a higher offer. A woman resisting the advances of some amorous swain might find it convenient to have a regular – and rather muscular – boyfriend to ring up at a pivotal moment.

And, of course, it provided a wonderful service for adulterers. That section of society whose activities had already been curtailed by the introduction of the itemized phone bill and the technology that enabled the location of a mobile phone call to be pinpointed (not from the fictional conference in Lytham St Annes but from the real Travelodge in Basildon) hugely welcomed Armitage Shanks's innovation. Thanks to the talents of his staff, the call from the adulterer's office to his home saying he'd have to go to the fictional conference in Lytham St Annes was perfectly convincing to whoever answered the phone. Indeed, adulterers who used to get paranoid about such subterfuges grew rather blasé and skilled at saying to their wives when the phone rang, 'Oh, could you get that, darling?'

So it was no surprise that through *SomeoneAtTheOther EndOfTheLine.com*, Mrs Pargeter, that afternoon in Gizmo Gilbert's front room, was able to access exactly the service she required.

She had assured her host that his invention (for which she gently suggested a better name might be 'The Zipper Zapper') was brilliant, innovative and essential for the contemporary woman, whether widowed or not. But also that, given the prevalence of industrial espionage, it was essential that his copyright in the idea should be asserted as soon as possible. The world was full of conscienceless villains who would like nothing better than to steal an idea of such genius.

She therefore, while still with him, rang through to the phone line of *SomeoneAtTheOtherEndOfTheLine.com*. When offered a sequence of numbered options, she keyed in the one that put her through to the Legal Department. She then accessed someone who was allegedly an expert in patents' law (though who'd, in fact, not worked at all since playing the back part of the pantomime horse in *Jack and the Beanstalk* at Colchester the previous Christmas).

The great beauty of the *SomeoneAtTheOtherEndOfTheLine. com* system was that the person in the same room as the caller – in this case Gizmo Gilbert – could hear just enough of the conversation for it to sound legitimate, but not enough for them to be able to pick up on the details.

So when, on concluding the call, Mrs Pargeter told him that she had done the deal, he had no reason to disbelieve her.

And when she told Gizmo Gilbert that the patent on 'The Zipper Zapper' had been registered and that he would receive by the next post a cheque for twenty-five thousand pounds (apparently from the Patent Office) as an advance against royalties on sales of the device, he could see no argument for refusing the money.

He insisted that Mrs Pargeter should put in her bag and keep the prototype of 'The Zipper Zapper' as a souvenir of a very serendipitous afternoon.

As she went round the corner to meet up with Gary in the Skoda Octavia, Mrs Pargeter congratulated herself on having been quite subtle.

THREE

Mrs Pargeter was a great believer in tea. Not just as a beverage, but in its more elaborate form as Afternoon Tea, as a meal. In fact, she was a great believer in all meals. The late Mr Pargeter had undertaken the education of her taste buds, as he had trained her in so many other aspects of life.

And in Mrs Pargeter's view the best Afternoon Tea in the world was served in the Blenheim Room of Greene's Hotel in London. Elegantly set in Mayfair, Greene's was seamlessly managed by a gentleman called Mr Clinton (who no longer liked being addressed as 'Hedgeclipper' Clinton, the nickname he'd had when he worked for the late Mr Pargeter. The reason why he had been called Hedgeclipper was something nobody had ever thought polite to ask). Though Mrs Pargeter was the owner of a recently completed and very extensive mansion in Essex, when she needed to stay in London she invariably took a room in Greene's.

These occasions caused the only rifts that ever appeared in her relationship with Hedgeclipper Clinton. Like Gary, the manager was very reluctant to charge Mrs Pargeter for the services that she enjoyed . . . 'when I think of everything your late husband did for me.' She occasionally had to get uncharacteristically firm – not to say cross – with both Gary and Hedgeclipper about their unwillingness to provide her with bills and invoices. Her late husband had been a businessman, and he had relied on those former associates, whom he set up in their careers, to behave like businessmen too.

Forewarned by her reservation, Hedgeclipper Clinton ensured that he was waiting at reception to greet Mrs Pargeter as she stepped out of Gary's Bentley at the Greene's Hotel doors on Monday afternoon. He rushed effusively towards her. 'Good afternoon, my dear Mrs Pargeter,' he said in the voice into which he had put a lot of work when he'd changed careers and gone into the hotel business. He had done a good job. Only in moments of extreme stress was a hint of his original Cockney allowed to emerge. And Hedgeclipper Clinton's unflappable urbanity ensured that he very rarely experienced moments of extreme stress. So most of the time his voice oozed class like butter melting on toast.

'Now, you will, of course, have your usual table in the Blenheim Room?'

'Thank you, Hedge – er, Mr Clinton.'

'My pleasure. And just the one guest, I gather.'

'Yes, Samantha Pinkerton. Actually, she's the daughter of Passport Pinkerton.'

Hedgeclipper Clinton's face instantly blanked over. 'I'm afraid I'm not familiar with anyone of that name.'

Mrs Pargeter was used to that reaction. Many of her late husband's associates suffered unexplained moments of memory loss about the times when they had worked for him. And even she had on occasion found herself being selective in her recollections of the past.

'Anyway, I'm afraid Passport Pinkerton has died.'

'How very regrettable for his family.' The hotel manager's response was no more than a formal acknowledgement of the death of someone he didn't know. 'Allow me to see you to your table, Mrs Pargeter.'

The Blenheim Room, like most of the public areas of Greene's, looked more like part of a stately home than anything so vulgarly commercial as a hotel. A few distinguished looking guests of various nationalities who were sitting there glanced up at the new arrival. They were impressed. She must be someone really important. *They* hadn't been guided to their seats by the hotel manager.

'I will arrange for your tea to be delivered forthwith, Mrs Pargeter,' said Hedgeclipper before beating an obsequious retreat.

She looked round the room with satisfaction. The mirrored walls, curtained with great swags of green velvet, were modelled on the interior of some French chateau, which had also supplied the inspiration for the huge chandelier hanging from the middle of the ceiling.

As ever, Mrs Pargeter felt perfectly at her ease. Growing up in Essex as a child she had never entertained the idea that rank or money might make anyone superior to her. And the generous lifestyle she had shared with her late husband meant that she was never fazed by the splendour of any hotel or restaurant. Mrs Pargeter was, as the French put it, 'comfortable in her skin' – and she had a splendidly lavish amount of skin to be comfortable in.

The tea had just arrived and two waiters were still setting up the display of silver cutlery and cake-stands when Hedgeclipper Clinton ushered in her guest. Samantha Pinkerton was a thin pretty girl in her early twenties. Her sloe-black eyes and dark hair suggested some Mediterranean input into her family history. The hair was centrally parted and flowed luxuriantly down to her shoulders. She wore a plain but well-cut dress in navy-blue cotton. She wore no jewellery except for a thin silver engagement band on her wedding finger.

Formally, she offered her hand to be shaken. 'Mrs Pargeter, it's very good to see you.' Her voice was pure, unreconstructed Essex.

'No problem, love. You take a seat.' When the girl was safely ensconced and cups of tea had been poured, Mrs Pargeter went on, 'I was very sorry to hear about your father's death.'

Samantha nodded, and there was a glint of a tear in her eye. The memory of her loss was still raw.

'Has the funeral happened?'

'Yes, well, it was just a quick do in a crematorium. Not many people, really, apart from me.'

'Oh, that's a pity. I would have thought some of his colleagues, who used to work for my husband, would have been there.'

'I don't think they knew about it. Dad did kind of cut himself off from everyone when he went to Spain.'

'Ah. Well, I'm sorry. We could've helped him out, I'm sure . . . if only we'd known where he was.'

'I'm afraid that's water under the bridge, really.'

'Yes. And did you pay for the funeral, Samantha?'

'Call me "Sammy", please.'

'Of course, Sammy. But did you pay for it?'

'Yeah. Just about cleaned me out, I'm afraid.'

'Have you got a job?'

'I did have. Worked in a retail outlet, but the last two, three years . . . well, I just been looking after Dad. Didn't have time to go out to work. I must sort something out soon.'

'So what did you live on?'

The girl grimaced. 'I had some savings. And my boyfriend, Kelvin, he chipped in a lot out of his . . . well, the money he had, until I . . .' She was straying into an area she didn't want to talk about and redirected herself. 'We managed . . . Don't know how, but we did. In that sense it was good Dad died when he did. Just got to the end of my savings. Don't know how we'd have managed much longer.' Something prompted a painful memory. The girl took a handkerchief out of her sleeve and pressed it to her face.

'I'm sorry,' said Mrs Pargeter again. 'And where do you live?'

'Kelvin and I got a flat in Southend.'

'Lovely,' said Mrs Pargeter. And she meant it. She had very pleasant memories of times spent in Southend with the late Mr Pargeter.

'Well, we got the flat as long as we can keep finding the rent.'

'Something'll come up.'

The girl smiled gratefully through her tears, not knowing that Mrs Pargeter had already decided that she was the something that would come up. 'I hope you're right. The trouble is that during the last years, when I was looking after my dad, though I got very close to him, there were still lots of things he didn't want to talk about.'

'Like what?'

'Like his early career, what he did before he went out to Spain.'

'Ah. I might be able to help there.'

'What d'you mean? Did you know him back then?'

'No, I never had the pleasure of meeting him, but I'm sure,' said Mrs Pargeter, thinking of the little black book, 'that I know people who did.'

'Well, anything you can find out . . .'

'Leave it with me,' said Mrs Pargeter with a comforting grin.

'Thank you,' said the girl, though her eyes were still sparkly with tears.

'Look, you haven't eaten anything,' said her hostess, who believed that most human predicaments could be alleviated by food. 'Have one of these cakes. They're really delicious.'

'I will in a minute,' the girl mumbled through her handkerchief as she tried to stem the flow of tears.

Mrs Pargeter allowed her to have her cry out. It didn't take long. Sammy wiped her nose in a businesslike way and returned the hanky to her sleeve. 'Sorry about that.'

'Don't apologize. I'm always in favour of a good cry when that's what you need,' Mrs Pargeter said, though she herself had never been seen to cry in public. She proffered a plate towards Sammy. 'Have an eclair. I always find an eclair's the solution to most problems. And Greene's pastry chef makes the best eclairs in the whole wide world.'

The girl took one and immediately bit into it. Finishing her mouthful, she said, 'You're right. That's bloody marvellous.'

'You talked about your boyfriend, Kelvin . . .'

'Yes. Well, he's my fiancé, actually.'

'Congratulations. And does that mean "fiancé" in the sense of someone you're going to get married to?'

The dark eyes looked puzzled. 'What else might it mean?'

'I'm sorry, Sammy, but these days one does have to ask. Lots of young people seem to get engaged without any intention of getting married for years and years.'

'No, Kelvin and I definitely want to get married. As soon as possible.'

'Sad that your dad won't be around to give you away.'

'Well, yes, I suppose it is. Though in one way it makes it easier.'

'Oh?'

'Dad didn't approve of Kelvin.'

'Oh dear.' Mrs Pargeter decided to hold back the question about what elements of the young man's character were disapproved of.

'In fact, Kelvin only asked me to marry him after Dad died.

I don't think he'd have done it while the old man was still around.'

'And Kelvin is the right one for you? You're sure of that?'

'Absolutely sure.' A large smile spread across the girl's dark features. 'I adore him. I can't wait to become Mrs Stockett.'

'Wonderful. Have you got a date for the wedding?'

'Yes, in about a month's time. Twenty-seventh of May.'

'Going to be a big do?'

'I wish,' the girl replied glumly. 'We'll just about manage to scrape together enough for the registrar's fees and the certificate.'

'Doesn't your fiancé, Kelvin, have a job?'

'Not exactly, no.' A blush suffused her pretty face. 'Anyway, I don't want to take money from him.'

'Why ever not?'

'Well . . .'

The girl was clearly unwilling to answer, and again Mrs Pargeter didn't press the point. Instead, she said, 'Look, I have a proposition to put to you, Sammy. I'm sorry I wasn't able to help your dad while he was alive, but at least there's something I can do to help you now.'

'What?'

'I will pay for your wedding.'

'You mean, the registrar's fees and everything? That's very kind of—'

'No, no, no. You don't really want to get married in a registry office, do you?'

'Well, it's all we can afford, and—'

'I told you, Sammy, I'm paying for everything.'

'Yes, but we've got the registry office booked and finding another venue at short notice would be—'

Mrs Pargeter waved away the objection. 'Most things can be sorted out at short notice when you know the right people. So you go ahead and plan the wedding you've always wanted. Church, flowers, bridesmaids, a hundred and fifty guests. And a really good hen party, too. Whatever you want. You plan it, and I'll pick up the tab.'

'Ooh, Mrs Pargeter!' The girl was clearly ecstatic at the news. 'But are you sure?'

'Never been surer about anything. It's what my late husband would have wanted. He was a great philanthropist, and he left me with more than enough money to continue his good work.'

'That's wonderful. I can never thank you enough. Is there anything I can do for you in return?'

'Yes, there is one thing . . .'

'Oh?'

'Invite me to the wedding, so that I can see you on the happiest day of your life.'

'Of course we'll do that. And you must come to the hen party too.'

'Oh, you don't want me there for—'

'I very definitely do. You must come.'

'Well, bless you, Sammy. And if you need any help with the planning   finding a venue, buying the dress, all that stuff – I'd be happy to help.'

'I might well take you up on that, Mrs Pargeter.'

'Do. I love weddings.' She held the plate out. 'I think we should both have another eclair to celebrate.'

They did, and ate in reverent silence to the last delicious dollop of cream.

Then Mrs Pargeter said, in a purely conversational tone, 'You said your father disapproved of your fiancé. Why was that?'

'It was to do with what Kelvin does for a living.'

'And what is that?'

'He's a criminal.'

FOUR

I t was later that Monday evening when the phone rang in Mrs Pargeter's large mansion near Chigwell. The house had been the dream home of her and the late Mr Pargeter. He had earmarked the plot of land and bought it, but sadly died before the project could reach completion. Sadly, before it had even reached commencement.

And, though Mrs Pargeter had been very keen to get the house built – as, amongst other things, a memorial to their marriage – she had encountered a lot of delays along the way. These had been caused chiefly by her choice of builder. There was nothing wrong with his professional skills – 'Concrete' Jacket was universally acknowledged as one of the best in the business – but he did have an unfortunate habit of getting on the wrong side of the law. Indeed, on one occasion when Mrs Pargeter had been visiting the site of her new home a body had been discovered, and Concrete Jacket found himself arrested for murder. Though he had been on that occasion exonerated, he had an unfortunate habit of committing other peccadillos, which led to his spending a certain number of extended periods at the pleasure of Her Majesty. As a result, the building of Mrs Pargeter's dream home had been a slow and laborious process.

But it was a magnificent dream. Built in Georgian proportions, the house had six bedrooms, every amenity that modern technology could supply and one and a half acres of garden. This last was attended to by a full-time gardener. Part of the late Mr Pargeter's dream of retirement had been spending more time getting dirt under his fingernails in the garden, but his widow's priorities were very different. Though she liked her surroundings to look nice, she had always found gardening deeply tedious. And throughout most of her life she had managed very effectively to steer clear of things she found tedious.

That evening Gary had brought her straight back from Greene's Hotel after her tea, and in the Bentley they had discussed the plight of Samantha Pinkerton. Gary had said he could definitely provide the cars for the wedding. 'Can do you a very good deal on them, Mrs P.' Which had, of course, prompted her knee-jerk reaction that he must charge his regular rates and give her a proper invoice for his services.

The evening caller on the telephone was Truffler Mason. 'Good to see you at the funeral, Mrs P,' he said in his customary voice of doom.

'You too, Truffler. Always good to see you.'

'And I've heard from Gizmo Gilbert. You done a lovely job there, Mrs P. Haven't compromised his pride at all. In fact, you've even made him prouder. He thinks you really have sorted out royalty payments on his "Zipper Zapper".'

'Well, I have,' protested Mrs Pargeter, relieved that Gizmo had gone along with her suggestion for the name of his latest invention.

'Oh yeah?'

'Yes. The cheque he received came from the Patent Office, didn't it?' she asked innocently.

From the other end of the line came a low lugubrious chuckle. Truffler was glad to hear that Mr Pargeter's widow was *au fait* with the large number of bank accounts her late husband had set up, which could apparently generate cheques from all kinds of public bodies.

'I've got the prototype of the "Zipper Zapper" and all, Truffler,' Mrs Pargeter continued righteously. 'I'm sure it'll come in useful one day.'

'Yes, I'm sure it will,' he said sceptically.

'And incidentally, thank you for setting up my meeting with Sammy Pinkerton.'

'Nice kid, isn't she?'

'Oh yes.' And Mrs Pargeter gave a brief résumé of her afternoon's philanthropy. But she didn't mention the criminal career of Sammy's fiancé. Though Truffler Mason was totally trustworthy, Mrs Pargeter wanted to find out a bit more about Kelvin's activities before she shared the knowledge with anyone else.

Then Truffler moved on to the purpose of his call: 'It's funny – it's connected, in a way, with the funeral.'

'Oh?'

'I had a call this morning from Lady Winthrop.'

'What did she want?'

'She wanted to employ me.'

'As a private investigator?'

'Of course. That's how I'm listed in all the directories. And OK, she may just have stumbled on my name by chance, but it did seem rather a coincidence . . . you know, with me having worked for your husband and her old man having done the same.'

'Having *possibly* done the same. We still have no proof of the connection.'

'But I'm sure we'll find it, Mrs P.'

'Hm. Anyway, did Lady Winthrop say what she wanted you to investigate?'

'No, she's coming to the office tomorrow afternoon to tell me about it.'

'Hm. That is odd, isn't it? You'll keep me posted about what she says, won't you?'

''Course I will, Mrs P. I'll put money on the fact that it has something to do with her husband's past.'

'Are you *certain* you never came across Sir Normington Winthrop in his earlier incarnation?'

'Never heard of him. And, of course, there was no mention of him working for your husband in the obituaries.'

'Well, there wouldn't be, would there?'

'No, I suppose not.'

'Incidentally, Truffler, I only read the obituary in the *Daily Mail*. Could you send me any others you've got?'

''Course. I'll email them straight away.'

'Thank you.' Mrs Pargeter did not use a computer a great deal, but she certainly knew how to download email attachments. She was thoughtful for a moment. 'I'd be interested to know a bit more about Sir Normington Winthrop's background. Pity "Jukebox" Jarvis is no longer with us.'

She referred to a small bespectacled man who got his nickname from the fact that he used to 'keep the records' of all the late Mr Pargeter's business activities. He was a computer expert who operated out of a terraced house in North London, where his office was a cat's cradle of wires and leads linking his accumulation of computer hardware. Among his many technical skills was the ability to hack in at will to police emails and thus secure invaluable advance notice of their plans.

Sadly, though, Jukebox Jarvis had died the previous year. Though Mrs Pargeter herself had been unable to attend, there had been a good turnout for his funeral of names from the little black book, but she rather feared that all his expertise had died with him. She expressed this regret to Truffler Mason and was much relieved by his reply.

'No, I worried about that for a bit, but then I had a call from his daughter, Erin. She's taken over the whole caboodle. Brought it up to date and all. 'Cause when I watched Jukebox doing his stuff, I reckoned he was a real whizz on the old computers. But Erin tells me technology's advanced a lot, and she's tidied up the records and put them on a much more modern system. I went to see her, and she's done wonderful stuff, digitized all the archive.'

'But would she have the stuff going right back to when my husband started his career?'

'I reckon she has got it all, yeah.'

'And are you sure she can be trusted?'

Truffler sounded almost affronted by the question. 'She's as trustworthy as her dad was. As to whether she's got all the stuff, I'll check with her tomorrow.'

'Oh?'

'I've fixed to see Erin, Mrs P, so's I've got a bit of background stuff on Lady Winthrop for when I meet up with her in the afternoon.'

'So you're actually going to Erin's house?'

'Yes, she still lives in her dad's place. Little terrace up North London way.'

'Ooh,' said Mrs Pargeter, greatly enthused. 'Do you mind if I come with you, Truffler?'

Rather than reading the obituaries that Truffler had sent her off the screen of her laptop, Mrs Pargeter printed them

out and read them in bed to the accompaniment of a large
Armagnac.

As anticipated, there was no mention of Sir Normington
Winthrop having dealings with her late husband. But he'd
clearly had a very distinguished career in public life, been a
man of great wealth and influence. Through all the sycophantic
flannel in the obituaries it was possible to work out that his
speciality had been the arms trade. Though never a member
of any government, he had acted as a consultant to many
governments, because of his unrivalled range of international
contacts, particularly in the Middle East.

And although the international arms trade had a justified
reputation for dodgy dealings, at no time during his career
had any aspersion been cast on the integrity of Sir Normington
Winthrop.

The one detail of his life that Mrs Pargeter had not known
about was his political affiliation. Though he had made himself
indispensable to governments both Labour and Tory, it was
not one of the mainstream parties that had claimed Winthrop's
allegiance. A time when only a few cigarette papers of policy
difference seemed to separate the two main contenders gave
the opportunity for minority groups to claim public attention,
and the one in which Sir Normington Winthrop had interested
himself was called BROG.

This acronym stood for 'Britons, Restore Our Greatness',
and it was just the kind of jingoistic set-up to flourish in the
aura of political uncertainty between general elections. BROG
was really a one-man band. Though it claimed to have many
other members, the only one to have any public recognition
was its founder – part tub-thumping populist, part buffoon –
who was known as Derek Bardon.

An instinctive self-publicist, Bardon was just the sort of
character that the tabloids thrived on. Though woolly on the
details of BROG's policies, he was a master of the political
stunt and adept at snatching headlines from the two main party
leaders. Derek Bardon had the huge advantage over them that
whereas promises *they* made might at some point have to be
put into action, there was no danger of that ever happening
with any promise made by BROG.

So though the party seemed never likely to achieve a representative at Westminster – or even an MEP – it did provide a
welcome focus for the grumbling middle-aged middle class
who reckoned they had through their lives watched the inevitable process of the once great Britain 'going to the dogs' (or,
in some saloon bars where such moans were expressed, 'to
hell in a handcart').

In the attitudes of BROG's members there was a dangerous
tendency against immigration, which at times strayed into
racism, but that was massaged by the party's publicity. Their
literature tended to concentrate on a nostalgic view of a Great
Britain which never probably existed: a land of warm beer
and village cricket, of cheery plough boys and rosy-cheeked
wenches sipping cider on haystacks.

For most of the country BROG was a joke. But clearly it
hadn't been for Sir Normington Winthrop. He had been a great
admirer of Derek Bardon and had, virtually on his own, funded
the party's growth. There was also the implication that the
terms of his will would continue that substantial funding.

Mrs Pargeter, who had always valued principle over politics,
found this new insight into the dead man very interesting.
But it wasn't the kind of thing that she would allow to keep
her awake, so after her regular loving goodnight to the photo
of her late husband on the bedside table, she settled down to
sleep.

The second phone call she had that evening, just after she had
turned out the light, was considerably less pleasant than the
earlier one she'd received from Truffler Mason.

'Mrs Pargeter?' asked a cultured voice which sounded
vaguely familiar.

'Yes.'

'My name is Edmund Grainger. We met at Sir Normington
Winthrop's funeral.'

'I remember. In fact, given your bad manners on that occasion,
I am hardly likely to forget.'

'Never mind my manners. I just want to know whether Lady
Winthrop has been in touch with you since the funeral?'

'No, and since you prevented me from speaking to her on

that occasion, it's hardly surprising, is it? She doesn't know me from Adam – or perhaps I should say Eve?'

'And has she been in touch with your associates – you know, the scruff-bags who were at the funeral with you?'

'What business would that be of yours, Mr Grainger?'

'Never mind. Has she been in touch with them?'

There was no way Mrs Pargeter was about to repeat what Truffler Mason had told her, so she lied succinctly: 'No.'

'Well, if any of them are approached by her, tell them to refuse to speak to her.'

'And why should I do that?'

He couldn't come up with anything more inventive than the threat he'd used after the funeral. 'Because if you don't it'll be the worse for you,' he hissed.

'Oh?'

'Mrs Pargeter, there are very important things at stake here.'

'Maybe if you were to tell me what those important things are, I might take your blustering a bit more seriously.'

'Just take my word for it. If you or any of your associates have any contact with Lady Winthrop, you will upset a lot of people who don't like being upset.'

'Can you be a bit more specific, Mr Grainger? If you're trying to frighten me, then I'm afraid your threats are too vague to have any such effect.'

'All right. Let's just say that if you have any contact with Lady Winthrop, you're in serious danger of getting yourself killed. Is that specific enough for you?'

Mrs Pargeter was not easily frightened. And at the end of the phone call she felt more curiosity than fear. Why was Edmund Grainger behaving in that manner? What was he afraid Lady Winthrop might say?

Or was it the other way round? Was he worried about something Mrs Pargeter or one of her associates might tell Lady Winthrop?

It was bizarre. And a little unsettling. Edmund Grainger had had no difficulty finding her number. And he'd used the landline. Which probably meant he knew where she lived.

Mrs Pargeter's first instinct was to ring Truffler Mason and tell him about the call. But something stopped her. She thought that Edmund Grainger was just a bully. And she'd never allowed herself to be intimidated by bullies. She was of the view that they were social inadequates who were all talk. To tell anyone about the phone call she'd just ended would mean that this particular bully had won. And she wasn't going to let him win.

FIVE

The following morning, as Gary piloted the Bentley towards the house in Chigwell an annoyingly familiar sequence of thoughts replayed through his head. His admiration for Mrs Pargeter had been strong from the moment he first met her, but he worried that his feelings had developed beyond mere admiration.

His track record with relationships wasn't great. For a time he'd felt settled. His most recent wife had been Denise, and that marriage had seemed promising. They'd lived together in a beautiful country cottage with a huge barn, where he'd parked all the vehicles when he'd started his car hire business. And that had seemed really promising . . . for a while.

But then he'd made the same mistake he'd made on so many other occasions. Started an affair with another woman. And had been careless enough to let Denise find out about it.

Sometimes he worried whether there was a kamikaze element in all his relationships. Just when everything was going fine, just when he should have been feeling secure, he'd go and do something to ruin the whole set-up. And that something was usually another woman. It had happened too often to be a coincidence.

The previous evening had seen the break-up of yet another in the long line of unsatisfactory relationships which had followed his divorce from Denise. It wasn't that the girls he habitually consorted with weren't pretty, weren't sexy, weren't entirely suitable partners for a man like him. It was just that they all seemed so young, so . . . callow (though that was probably not a word that Gary knew).

Basically, they all seemed so immature when compared to Mrs Pargeter.

Deep down he knew he didn't stand a chance with her. It wasn't that he was unattractive – the ease with which he picked up women he didn't care about suggested the very opposite.

And he couldn't have wished for more affection and concern for his welfare from Mrs Pargeter. But he knew the unlikelihood, indeed impossibility, of his feelings for her ever being reciprocated. She had enjoyed the perfect relationship with the late Mr Pargeter and, rather than settle for anything less, was determined to live out her widowhood in solitary philanthropy.

She was totally unaware of what Gary felt for her. And in many ways he knew that that was the right situation – indeed, the idea of his making some declaration to her was acutely embarrassing and could only sour their relationship. But he did still feel on occasion the need to present her with some token of his unspoken feelings.

Hence the parcel on the back seat of the Bentley.

'Oh, it's lovely,' said Mrs Pargeter as she unwrapped the life-size china figurine of a pink and white cat with gold details on its nose, whiskers and feet. Though she was a woman who preferred always to say what she thought, she knew there were moments when honesty should be tempered with tact.

'I'm really glad you like it, Mrs P,' said Gary, a raspberry blush suffusing his cheeks. 'The moment I saw the thing, I knew it had your name written all over it.'

This wasn't the time for her to say he had just demonstrated how little he knew her. Instead, she uttered some bland platitude about how thoughtful he was, already planning in the depths of which cupboard she would hide the thing when she was next alone in the house.

Amongst the many insights her late husband had taught her had been an appreciation of the beauty – and value – of artworks, and she had instantly recognized that Gary's gift had no aesthetic quality at all.

Also, it was a cat – and a cat of the most winsome kind. Though of a very generous nature, Mrs Pargeter had never become sentimental over pets. Unlike the majority of people in the British Isles, she believed there were enough human beings in the world who needed her help before she got round to starting on the animal kingdom.

But Gary's next words rather took the wind out of her sails. 'I chose it specially because I thought it would go so well on

the mantelpiece in here . . . you know, picking up the blues
in the wallpaper.'

This undoubtedly presented a difficulty. Mrs Pargeter had
spent a lot of time and thought on the decor of her new home
once Concrete Jacket had finally completed it, and in no way
did a pink, white and gold china cat fit in with her plans. Least
of all on the mantelpiece of her sitting room, whose chief
feature was a very fine and sober photograph of her late
husband.

But Mrs Pargeter had a soft heart and, before she and
Gary left in the Bentley, the cat was duly installed on her
mantelpiece.

And as they drove to pick up Truffler Mason, she wondered
how to convey to her cleaning lady the message that an inad-
vertent sweep of the duster, which brought the china cat down
to smash on the marble hearthstone, would not be greeted as
entirely bad news.

The suburban terraced house looked unostentatious, respect-
able, even dull, as Gary's Bentley drew up outside. 'Shall I
wait in the car?' Gary asked.

'No,' said Truffler. 'You should come and meet Erin. She's
a great kid.'

Gary looked for permission to Mrs Pargeter, who said, 'Yes,
the more the merrier.'

The girl who opened the door to them was dressed in black,
almost punk-like but with a style of her own. Her hair was
asymmetrically cut and coloured purple. Her ears had more
perforations than a tea bag, and from each hole hung a small
silver ring.

Truffler Mason was clearly very impressed by her. His
manner as he made the introductions was proudly avuncular,
almost proprietorial.

Mrs Pargeter said appropriate things about Jukebox Jarvis's
death.

'Yes, I was sorry to see him go,' said Erin. 'But he was in
so much pain towards the end . . . Well, it was probably for
the best. Now do come through and let me get you some tea
or coffee.'

It was clear as she led them through to the office that not just the management but also the style of Jukebox Jarvis's operation had changed considerably. Truffler and Gary both remembered the spaghetti junction chaos of cables in which he worked, the eviscerated boxes of computer parts, the piles of CDs, the profusion of printers.

But now Erin Jarvis was in charge all of that had vanished. The room had been painted in pale grey and charcoal. The shelves were minimally decorated with small ceramic vases, each one exquisitely different and selected with enormous care. A sleek-looking Italian coffee-making machine stood out among the ceramics. There were flowers in evidence and easy chairs covered in dark-grey fabric. A black leather swivel chair faced a glass-topped table which served as a desk. On it sat a solitary laptop. A wireless printer on a shelf was the only other evidence that this was a working environment.

Reading their reactions to the room from their faces, Erin said to Truffler and Gary, 'It's the technology that's changed, you see. Dad hoarded stuff, a lot of it still in old cardboard files. Then, his hardware wasn't really state of the art, so he did need lots of different computers for different tasks. Now I can do the whole lot from the one.'

Erin sat them down and took their coffee orders. While the machine hissed and gurgled, Mrs Pargeter asked, 'Have you got the whole archive on that one laptop?'

Erin nodded. 'Yes, I've got it backed up elsewhere – you know, on memory sticks and the cloud and so on – but it's all accessible from there.'

'Amazing. But how do you know where to find stuff? If the archive covers the whole of my husband's business career, a lot of it must go back to before you were born.'

'It does. But my dad took me through it all, you see.'

'How'd you mean?'

'Well, when it was pretty clear he was going to die – he had cancer which was spreading like mad – he said it'd be a waste of his life's work if the Mr Pargeter archive wasn't saved. Because it was all there, but in such a disorganized way that Dad was the only person who could navigate his way around it. Well, I'd got a degree in IT studies – Dad had seen to it I had a good education – so it seemed only natural that I should work with him, digitalizing everything and getting it into a kind of order where it was more accessible. We spent his last six months doing that. And the day after we'd finished, Dad died. I think he'd been kind of holding himself together till we got it done.'

'I'm sorry,' said Mrs Pargeter gently.

'No, don't be. It was the best six months of my life. It gave me a chance to get really close to Dad . . . in a way I never had before. I wouldn't have missed a day of it.'

The girl looked proud and confident. Mrs Pargeter couldn't help comparing her to Samantha Pinkerton. Sammy's grief about her father's death was still raw, but Erin Jarvis had reached an accommodation with the reality of it, a kind of peace.

The thought prompted her next question: 'So you'd be able to look up anyone who worked with my husband?'

'Should be able to. Who did you have in mind?'

'Well, I've recently met the daughter of a bloke called Passport Pinkerton, and she'd really like to find out about his early career.'

'I think I could manage that.' Erin keyed in a note on the tablet on her desk.

'I'll give you her number, then maybe you can ring her when you've got some stuff together . . .?'

'No problem.'

Mrs Pargeter scribbled down the name and mobile number and passed it across. 'Going back to your archive, Erin,' she said. 'Presumably, you didn't get paid for doing any of this?'

'No, it was a labour of love. Literally. Love for my dad.'

'Maybe so, but it's still a very valuable piece of work. Valuable for me, to know that all my husband's archives are in such excellent shape. I will see to it that you are paid for your efforts.'

'You really don't need to, Mrs Pargeter. I do have other sources of income.'

'Really? May I ask what they are?'

'Research, records, information. People employ me when they need to find out things.'

'What kind of things?' asked Mrs Pargeter a little tentatively. She hoped Erin Jarvis wasn't going to turn out to have criminal connections.

'Just data, really. Facts.'

Truffler Mason came in at this point. 'Erin provides a very useful service, of which I have already taken advantage. She's like a walking Google. Whatever you ask for, she'll be back with the answer within five minutes – or less. For instance, case I was working on, I needed to find out about adoption laws – at what age a kid can demand to know who her birth parents are. Erin was back with the answer, almost before I'd finished asking the question.'

'Oh, this does sound a very useful service, Erin.' Mrs Pargeter beamed at the girl. 'I'm sure I'll be in touch with some queries very soon indeed.'

'Great.' Erin picked up a card from the table and handed it across. 'All my contacts.'

'Thank you so much.'

The coffee was now ready, and Erin distributed it in stylish black cups. Then she sat down. 'Truffler mentioned on the phone this morning there was something to do with your husband's archive you might want me to check out . . .'

'Well, if you've got the time, yes there is. And not just the query about Passport Pinkerton. That was really an after-thought. The more important thing from my point of view is that we were recently at the funeral of Sir Normington Winthrop. Only reason I went there was because I'd found his name in an address book my husband left me – which contains details of all the people he ever worked with. I mean, I suppose it's possible that there was more than one Normington Winthrop and we went to the wrong funeral, but it's an unusual name.'

'Well,' said Erin, 'I can check out if there are any other Normington Winthrops.'

'How can you . . .?'

But the girl was already too involved to reply. Her fingers flittered across the keyboard, playing it like a piano virtuoso. In less than thirty seconds, she stopped and announced, 'There was a Major Normington-Winthrop who was killed in the Boer War, but that was his surname and he was hyphenated.'

'Was he? Poor bloke,' murmured Gary, and received a frosty reproof for levity from Mrs Pargeter's violet eyes.

'Then there was a Normington Stanley Winthrop whose funeral took place in Ketchum, Idaho in 1894. And there's a firm of estate agents in Edmonton called Normington, Patel & Winthrop.'

'Anything else?'

'Apart from a village in Dorset called Norton Windrop, no.'

'Well, thank you very much, Erin. I think we can definitely say that there is some connection between my husband and the man whose funeral we attended.'

'Seems likely, yes.'

'Still odd, though,' said Truffler, 'that neither Gary nor I have heard the name.'

'Perhaps not so odd. I get the impression that Normington Winthrop was with my husband right at the start of his operations, so you probably joined up after he'd left.'

'Yes, but why did he leave?' A new portentousness came into Truffler's voice. 'Your husband was such a good employer that nobody left . . . unless they left *under a cloud*.'

'You're right. Perhaps there is some history there . . . of Normington Winthrop trying to do the dirty on my husband. Would that possibly be recorded somewhere, Erin? I don't know if your records go back that far.'

'They seem to cover everything,' the girl replied with a grin. 'I get the impression that your husband kept very copious notes of his enterprises right from the beginning. Then he employed my dad to keep the records, and passed over all the early stuff to him.'

'Good.'

'But, Mrs Pargeter, what makes you think that Normington Winthrop was involved so early on in your husband's work?'

'Two things. One: as well as Truffler and Gary here, I've asked a few more of their associates, and none of them ever met him, though one or two seemed vaguely to remember the name. The second thing is the way Normington Winthrop is written down in the listings.' She extracted the little black book from her bag to illustrate the point. 'Look . . .' She flicked through the pages. 'My husband listed the names according to their individual expertise – "Missing Persons Investigators" and so on – and they're entered when they joined his organisation. So here you see "Normington Winthrop" is the first one entered in the "Armourers" category. Before "Half-inch" Warburton and "Winkler" Whittington and all the others. What's more, my husband always used a Parker Pen with an italic nib and Quink Royal Blue ink.'

'Lovely writing he had,' murmured Gary, looking at the book.

'Yes, he prided himself on his writing.'

'Can I just have a butcher's at that,' asked Truffler.

Mrs Pargeter passed the book across. He put on a pair of thick glasses and brought the page very near to his face. 'Funny, it's a bit messy, that. The way he's written "Normington Winthrop".'

'How do you mean?'

'Well, the paper looks a bit rough and the ink's run a bit, like it was smudged.'

'That's probably just because it's been there such a long time,' said Mrs Pargeter. 'Further proof that Normington Winthrop was one of the first people my husband recruited.'

'Yes.' Truffler Mason let out a low whistle of appreciation. 'I think I should give up this private detective lark, Mrs P. You're better at it than I am.'

'Very sweet of you to say so, Truffler, but what I did wasn't very difficult.'

'No, maybe not.'

'So what you want me to do,' said Erin, keen to be busy, 'is to find out whatever there is in the archive about Normington Winthrop?'

'Exactly. And how long do you reckon it'll take you, love? Couple of days?'

'Couple of minutes more like. Now, before I get started, is everyone all right for coffee?'

Everyone was all right for coffee, and as Erin focused on her laptop Gary asked, 'All right if we talk? Or will we spoil your concentration?'

'Nothing spoils my concentration,' said Erin.

'I was just thinking back, Truffler,' said Gary, 'to that job you and me done with Mr P in Stoke Newington.'

The private investigator let out a lugubrious chuckle. 'Stoke Newington – cor, that was a job and a half, wasn't it? 'Cause your getaway car seized up totally, didn't it?'

'Yeah, it went on unleaded, and some pranny had only filled it up with diesel, hadn't they?'

'Did you ever find out who did it?'

'No, and lucky for him. If I had found him, he wouldn't have sat down for a week.'

Truffler Mason chuckled again. 'What a nightmare! 'Cause there I was holding the sack from the building society, knowing their alarms'd be ringing like there's no tomorrow, and—'

'Well, be fair. I sorted it out, didn't I? I hijacked another vehicle.'

'Yes, but did it have to be a bloody milk float?'

That got both the men laughing uproariously. When they'd recovered, both looked at Mrs Pargeter. There was an unwonted frostiness in her violet eyes.

'Well, it was funny at the time,' said Gary limply. 'I guess you had to be there.'

'I have no idea,' said Mrs Pargeter, 'what on earth you're talking about.'

Further uncomfortable conversation was prevented by Erin suddenly saying, 'This is really odd.'

'What is?'

'There is absolutely no record anywhere in the archive of Normington Winthrop. Not even his name.'

'Maybe wires got crossed somewhere?' suggested Gary. 'Maybe he never did work for Mr P.'

'If that were the case,' said Mrs Pargeter firmly, 'his name wouldn't be in the little black book.' She looked across at Erin. 'Is there any possibility that the archive could have been tampered with?'

'Certainly not since I've had it on my computer. You wouldn't believe the levels of security I've got on this thing.'

'And you don't have any of the original records, do you? You know, the folders and notebooks whose contents you copied and digitized.'

'I have all of them. They're stored in the next room. There's so much stuff, I had to get some of those shelves on rollers fitted . . . you know, like you have in libraries.'

'But if you've been through all that material you'd have noticed if anything had been tampered with, wouldn't you?'

'Well, no. Dad did the very early stuff. First idea was, you see, that I should show him how to do it, and then he'd work through all of the material. So he made a start, but then the cancer got worse, with the result that I stepped in and we done the rest together.'

'So there might be evidence of tampering that you've never seen?'

'Possible, Mrs Pargeter, yes. I'll go and check.'

There was silence in the room until Erin Jarvis returned. Neither Truffler nor Gary wanted to initiate another topic of conversation that might prompt an icy stare from Mrs Pargeter's violet eyes.

Erin was quickly back with two notebooks, the pages of which crackled with age. She opened them to show the spaces where rectangles of text had been cut out. As she flicked through the pages, more and more excisions were revealed.

'It looks to me,' said Mrs Pargeter, 'as if Normington Winthrop has been airbrushed out of history.'

SIX

Though the main aim of the evening was to introduce Sammy's fiancé to Mrs Pargeter, the two women had agreed to meet in the bar of Greene's Hotel a little earlier to discuss wedding plans, a subject on which Sammy seemed unable to contain her enthusiasm.

She arrived on a bubble of excitement, with a sheaf of magazines under her arm. Mrs Pargeter had, of course, ordered a bottle of champagne, which was reclining luxuriously in an ice bucket. She was already halfway down a glass, and a member of the bar staff expertly filled another for her guest.

Mrs Pargeter raised hers. 'Thought you should taste the house champagne. Greene's does a very nice line in wedding receptions.'

Sammy's dark eyes widened. 'What, you mean we could have the do here?'

'Why not?'

'Well . . .' The girl took in the splendour of her surroundings. 'It'd cost an absolute fortune.'

'I've told you – you don't have to worry about the cost.'

'No, but . . .' Sammy's eyes did another tour of inspection and a slight apprehensiveness came into them. 'I'm not sure I'd ever feel really relaxed in a place like this.'

'No worries. It was just a suggestion. The important thing is that you have exactly the kind of wedding you want.'

'Yes.' Sammy took a sip of champagne. 'The fact is, Mrs Pargeter, I'm an Essex girl and . . .'

'Me too.' A warm chuckle. 'Takes one to know one, eh?'

'Yes. And there's a place near where I live . . . It's a wedding venue, you know; they do the whole package . . . I've been to lots of my friends' weddings there, and I always kind of dreamed that if I ever got married, that's the place where it'd happen.'

'Fine,' said Mrs Pargeter. 'If that's what you want, that's what you shall have. What's the place called?'

'Girdstone Manor.'

'Very well. I'll book it. Are you still hoping to get married on the twenty-seventh of May?'

'Hoping to, yes. But a place like Girdstone Manor gets booked up months in advance.'

'Well, we can check it out. They might have a cancellation.'

'Ooh, that'd be good.' Sammy's eyes sparkled, then she realized what she'd just said. 'Well, that is, it'd be good for Kelvin and me, but it would mean that some other poor girl's engagement had been broken off.'

'Sammy, there's no point in being sentimental about people you don't know. My husband used to say that to me a lot – and it was a very good indicator of how he ran his business.'

'Mm.'

'And presumably at Girdstone Manor you can have any kind of ceremony you like?'

'How d'you mean?'

'Well, I don't know if you've got any faith or not – whether you want a church wedding?'

'I don't know whether I've got any faith or not – and I'm sure Kelvin doesn't – but I do want a church wedding.'

'Good for you,' said Mrs Pargeter, who liked to keep some things traditional.

'I mean, it struck me, when we had Dad's funeral . . . you know, that the crematorium was a bit gloomy. I sort of wished we'd been able to do that in a church. So I would like a church wedding, yes. Lot of my friends who've got married at Girdstone Manor, they've gone for that too. Place has a tiny chapel in the grounds – the whole estate used to belong to some famous family, I think. And if you've got too many guests, they set up a marquee outside with closed circuit television, so everyone can enjoy the service.'

'And do they – the management at Girdstone Manor – supply a priest to do the business?'

'Yes.' A shadow crossed the girl's face. 'That's the one thing I wasn't so keen on. Three weddings I've been to there, and the same bloke's done them all. He sort of doesn't sound interested in what he's saying . . . like he was kind of ticking off items at a supermarket checkout. Still, I suppose that's only a minor thing.'

'No, it isn't. It's a very big thing. It's your wedding. You don't want it conducted by someone who finds the whole occasion a great big yawn. No, I'm sure the management at Girdstone Manor will let you bring in your own priest . . . you know, if it's a family member or a personal friend.'

'I'm afraid none of my family have ever been vicars, and I don't know any.' She read something encouraging in Mrs Pargeter's violet eyes. 'Why, do you?'

'Do you know, I think I might have just the perfect person. Leave it with me. Ooh, and if we're really going for the twenty-seventh of May, you'd better start getting the hen party sorted. It'll have to be soon, won't it?'

'Yes.'

'Let's make it this Saturday. Will that give your friends enough notice?'

'I'm sure it will. They won't want to miss it.'

'So what would you like to do for your hen party?'

'Well, go to a few clubs, I suppose.'

'In Essex or London?'

'London would be wonderful, but it'll be very expensive and—'

'London it is. Don't forget I'm paying. And we'll book all your friends in here for the night.'

'Here in Greene's Hotel?'

'Of course. I don't want them worrying about late-night taxis. And, actually, we could start the evening with dinner here. I like the idea of your friends having something solid in their stomachs before the serious drinking starts.'

'Mrs Pargeter, I don't know what to say.'

'"Thank you" is all that's required.'

'Thank you.'

'My pleasure.' Mrs Pargeter grinned, because it really was her pleasure. 'Anyway, what are all these magazines you've brought?'

Sammy fanned out the pile. 'These are all for brides – full of lots of clever ideas and stuff.'

It was a long time since Mrs Pargeter had had anything to do with wedding preparations – her own was the last in which she had been actively involved. That had been a very traditional and sedate affair; her late husband would not have wished for it to be any other way. Ceremony in a City of London church, reception in one of the City Livery Company halls, honeymoon on the island of Capri.

Since then, though she had attended a few, she hadn't given much thought to the subject of wedding planning, so she was amazed by the proliferation of magazines which Sammy held out to her. But that didn't mean she was not interested, and the two women spent a very happy half-hour looking at wedding dresses. The range on offer was enormous, though the list of potential candidates was considerably reduced by the fact that, unlike many of the models in the magazines, Sammy didn't want to get married looking like a meringue.

'I'm only just looking,' she said rather wistfully. 'Dresses like this have to be ordered months in advance.'

'Again,' said Mrs Pargeter with a sly wink, 'don't under-estimate what can be done at short notice.'

The first bottle of champagne was painlessly consumed and Mrs Pargeter had just ordered the second when Sammy's fiancé appeared in the bar. He was a tall, good-looking boy with floppy very fair hair and a dark suit, the one-size-too-small look of which was fashionable that year. From the expression on Sammy's face when he arrived it was clear that she absolutely adored him, and his eyes reflected matching enthusiasm.

Introductions were quickly made and glasses filled. Kelvin thanked Mrs Pargeter very formally for her generosity in offering to fund the wedding, but a restraint in his manner suggested he wasn't wholly pleased with the idea.

Mrs Pargeter was not a woman to let atmospheres build up. She had always been very quick to point out elephants in rooms, so she immediately asked, 'Aren't you happy about me footing the bill, Kelvin?'

'Well, it doesn't quite seem right. I feel we should be doing it.'

'There's no need to worry about it, love. The tradition with weddings is that the bride's parents pay, but a) that's very outdated, and b) Sammy's parents are both dead.'

'Yes, but—'

'Are your parents still alive, Kelvin?'

'No. My mother died about this time last year. And my father . . . nearly ten years ago now.' His mother's death was almost casually dismissed, but when the boy spoke of his father, it was clear from his manner that, like Sammy, he was still feeling the emotional impact of his loss.

'Well, I don't see why you've got a problem with me paying. For a start, I'm doing it as a kind of compensation for things that were neglected earlier, picking up my late husband's unfinished business. If I'd known what dire straits Sammy's Dad was in while he was alive, I'd have helped him out then. Sadly, I didn't, so this is a way of making up for that.'

'When you say "your late husband" . . .' A note of awe crept into the boy's voice. 'Are you talking about "Mr Pargeter"?'

'Well, yes, of course I am. My married surname is "Pargeter", so my husband was called "Mr Pargeter".'

'But was he *the* Mr Pargeter?'

'In certain circles he would be known as "*the* Mr Pargeter", yes.'

The boy reached across to take her hand. 'It's a great honour to meet you, Mrs Pargeter.'

'Nice to meet you and all, Kelvin. And now you know who my husband was, do you feel better about me paying for your wedding?'

'Well, yes, I suppose . . .' But the note of doubt was still in his voice.

'What's the problem now?'

'It's just . . .'

'What? We both want Sammy to have the wedding she's always dreamed of, don't we?'

'Yes, but I wanted to give her that. I wanted to pay for it!'

'Lovely idea, Kelvin, but you've got to face facts. Sammy says neither of you have got any money.'

'I've got lots of money!'

'Then why . . .?' Mrs Pargeter looked across at Sammy.

The girl was really tearing up. Clearly, the conversation had moved on to a topic of some disagreement between the young couple.

Sammy rose to her feet, clutching her handbag to her. 'I'm sorry. I must just . . . go to the ladies'.' And she hurried out of the bar, tears streaming down her face.

'What's this all about, Kelvin?' asked Mrs Pargeter.

'Well, look, like I say, I've got lots of dosh. I could pay for a slap-up wedding ten times over.'

'Oh. If you'd rather I didn't pay; if you really want to do it yourself . . .'

'I desperately want to do it myself, but Sammy won't let me.'

'How'd you mean?'

'She's totally skint, but she refuses to let me pay for anything for her.'

'Is that some kind of feminist thing?'

'No, it's because . . .' He built up to the confession. 'She doesn't like where my money comes from.'

'Ah. You mean because it's the proceeds of crime?'

'How did you know that? Did Sammy mention it?'

'She did, yes.'

'Anyway, the result is, she won't accept any money – or even any presents – from me. She says it's a matter of principle with her.'

'Well, she doesn't seem to love you any the less because of it.'

'Oh no, we adore each other. There's no problem there.'

'But disagreement over something so basic as where your money comes from could lead to problems later in your marriage.'

'I don't see why it should.'

'Maybe not, but . . . You want Sammy to be happy, don't you?'

''Course I do. I'd do anything for her.'

'Even the one thing that would really make her happy?'

'What's that?'

'Give up what you're doing now and get a proper legitimate job?'

He looked very shocked. 'Oh no, I couldn't possibly do that.'

'Why not?'

'Crime isn't just something I do . . .'

'Oh?'

'No. For me it's a vocation.'

SEVEN

Mrs Pargeter could cook. Indeed, during the years of her marriage she had hunted through recipe books to produce many fine meals for her husband. Though very loyal to his staff, Mr Pargeter had not been by nature a gregarious man, and those evenings he was free he generally preferred a peaceful meal at home with his wife to the public exposure of a restaurant. (Studies of New York's Little Italy had taught him what dangerous places restaurants could be.)

But Mrs Pargeter had no appetite for cooking elaborate dishes just for herself. When alone in the Chigwell mansion at a mealtime, she would assemble light snacks of smoked salmon, cold roast guinea fowl, oysters or caviar. But that didn't happen very often. As a general rule, she much preferred to go out to eat. There were half a dozen good restaurants in Chigwell that she frequented and a range of venues in central London (including, of course, Greene's Hotel) where she knew the menu by heart and was always welcomed enthusiastically by the manager and staff.

Mrs Pargeter didn't have any of those strange inhibitions some women do about eating on her own. For Mrs Pargeter, food was something to be enjoyed. She liked having company during a meal, but would not let its absence inhibit her from the deep relish she had for eating.

So when, just as she was about to leave Greene's after her encounter with Sammy and Kelvin, she got a phone call from Truffler Mason, eager to report on his afternoon's meeting with Helena Winthrop, it seemed logical to suggest he join her there for dinner. And since Gary had just arrived with the Bentley to take her home, it seemed equally logical to invite him too.

Mrs Pargeter and Truffler managed to demolish another bottle of champagne before going into the restaurant, where she was immediately led through to her favourite table. The waiters knew what she was likely to have – a salad of crayfish tails followed by a rare entrecôte steak with creamed spinach and matchstick potatoes – but they still went through the full business of ordering, a ceremony only slightly less elaborate than the coronation of an Eastern potentate.

Truffler and Gary went for steaks too, though their starters were whitebait and duck pâté respectively. From the wine list Mrs Pargeter selected a very good (and very expensive) bottle of Argentinian Malbec, which she and Truffler would share. Gary, aware of the risks to his business, was very good about not drinking when he was about to drive. And since he was always about to drive, he hardly ever drank.

'So, Truffler,' said Mrs Pargeter once the waiters had melted obsequiously away, 'what was Lady Winthrop after?'

'Well, it's very odd,' he replied dolorously. 'She wants me to do more or less exactly what we want to do.'

'How d'you mean?'

'She wants me to find out everything I can about the early career of her late husband, Sir Normington Winthrop.'

'Hm.'

'So I think that could be rather handy – doing a job I was going to do anyway and getting paid for it by a new client.'

'But I was going to pay you, Truffler.'

'Yes, I know, Mrs P, but now you don't have to.'

'I don't want anyone doing work on the cheap for me. I want full rates and proper invoices to be—'

'Oh, don't let's get into all that again, for Gawd's sake,' said Gary, to whom this was all too familiar. 'So, Truffler, Lady Winthrop doesn't know anything about his past then?'

'Well, she knows about his career since he became part of the establishment. I mean, he was already making his way in London society when she met him. But not how he started his career. Apparently, he never talked about that.'

'Surprise, surprise,' said Mrs Pargeter. 'Did she know about any connection between Sir Normington and my husband?'

'No. I didn't want to make too much of it, but I did mention the name Mr Pargeter, subtly, like, and she showed no reaction at all.'

'Did she say why she suddenly wanted to know all this stuff?'

'She gave me a lot about how the shock of losing her husband had made her realize there were gaps in her information about him, you know, and how she wished she'd talked to him more about that while she was alive. She even pretended to get quite emotional about it.'

'"Pretended"?'

'Yeah. She didn't fool me, Mrs P. She's one of those toffee-nosed women who had her emotions surgically removed at a very early age. Whatever the reason is that she wants to find out about her husband, sentimentality doesn't come into it.'

'So,' asked Gary, 'what do *you* reckon's the real reason why she suddenly wants you to check out her old man's background?'

'Well . . .' Truffler Mason stroked his chin thoughtfully. 'I kind of got the impression – don't know why, exactly – that she's doing it because of something someone said at the funeral.'

'You don't know who it was?' asked Mrs Pargeter. 'Or what they said?'

He shook his large horse-like head from side to side. 'No. Like I say, it was just an impression.'

'Hm.' Their starters had arrived. The waiters laid them down on the table like diamond necklaces on a jeweller's velvet and evaporated back to the kitchens.

'Before we start eating, Truffler . . .' Mrs Pargeter turned the full beam of her violet eyes on to him. 'You said Lady Winthrop had never heard of my husband . . .'

'Yes, I'm sure she hadn't.'

'But what about me? Had she heard of me?'

'Again, no. No reaction when I mentioned you.'

'Well, that's odd. Because at the funeral Edmund Grainger knew exactly who I was, didn't he?'

'Yes.'

'I think we need to find out a bit more about Mr Edmund Grainger.' She was tempted to tell them about the threatening phone call she had received, but stopped herself because she knew both men would immediately go into overdrive about her safety. And once again she was determined not to give in to bullying.

'I'll get on to it first thing in the morning,' said Truffler.

'And I'll give Erin a call 'n' all, see if she can get some gen on him.'

Truffler and Gary's forks, advancing towards their starters, were stopped by another question from Mrs Pargeter. 'Do you have any idea why Lady Winthrop chose your detective agency?'

'According to her, she just got out the *Yellow Pages* and virtually stuck a pin in it.'

'I wonder if that could be true,' said Mrs Pargeter thoughtfully. 'Her late husband had some connection with my late husband; you worked for my late husband; she stuck her pin into the *Yellow Pages* and contacted you. How d'you explain that?'

'Coincidence,' Truffler Mason offered without a lot of conviction.

'I'm not a great believer in coincidence,' said Mrs Pargeter. 'I always tend to look for an alternative explanation. And I very often find one.'

EIGHT

Though sceptical about coincidence, Mrs Pargeter was a great believer in both synchronicity and serendipity, so she was unsurprised by the successful outcome of the call she made the following morning, which was a Wednesday.

Although she could handle a computer and was quite capable of sending emails, she preferred to use the phone as a means of communication. When she could hear the voice of the person at the other end of the line, she could get so much more information from them than a printed message could provide. Every intonation, every hesitation, every tremble of the voice revealed something about the person she was speaking to.

And only minutes into her conversation with Shereen, the Bookings Manager at Girdstone Manor, Mrs Pargeter knew that she was speaking to someone very professional, but whose assumed affability reined in a very short temper.

Once Mrs Pargeter had identified herself, the Bookings Manager asked what she could do for her.

'I want to book a wedding.'

'Well, you've certainly come to the right place. The satisfaction rating from brides and grooms who have used our services is over ninety per cent.'

'I'm very glad to hear that.'

'Now, Mrs Pargeter, are we talking about a wedding for yourself or your daughter?'

She giggled. 'No, Shereen, it's certainly not for me. And I haven't got a daughter.'

A puzzled: 'Oh?'

'No, the bride is the daughter of a friend who sadly has recently passed away.'

'I'm so sorry,' came the formal response.

'I'm just checking out the availability of Girdstone Manor.'

'Well, I'd better warn you that because of our high reputation we are extremely popular, and often for summer dates

the booking has to be made as much as a year ahead, sometimes more.'

'What about people who don't like long engagements?'

'They would be well advised to look elsewhere. There are a
great number of other, inferior wedding venues around, where
I am sure the demand is not so great.'

'I was looking for a date within the next month.'

'Well, Mrs Pargeter,' said Shereen with considerable *hauteur*,
'I think you would be well advised to—'

'Saturday the twenty-seventh of May.'

'I can assure you that—' The Bookings Manager paused
for a moment, the wind truly taken out of her sails. 'Did you
say Saturday the twenty-seventh of May?'

'I did indeed.'

'What a remarkable coincidence.'

'I prefer to call it "serendipity",' said Mrs Pargeter. 'Go on,
tell me – you've had a cancellation?'

'Well, yes, we have. I'd just put the phone down to the poor
girl when you rang. She was in a terrible state.'

'What, had she just found out that her fiancé had been
sleeping with the chief bridesmaid?'

'How did you know that was it?'

'It usually is. So the twenty-seventh of May is currently
available?'

'Well, yes, it is.'

'Then I would like to book it, please, Shereen.'

'Yes, yes, of course, Mrs Pargeter. I should warn you there's
a rather substantial deposit required to . . .'

'Non-returnable?'

'Non-returnable,' Shereen confirmed.

'So you'll be hanging on to the deposit from the girl who
cried off, won't you?'

'Well, we—'

'Going to be a profitable day for you, twenty-seventh of
May, isn't it?'

'There are costs involved in a cancellation,' Shereen
responded rather sniffily. 'Some outside people booked for
the wedding – the registrar, musicians and so on – have to
be paid off.'

'My heart bleeds for you. Anyway, I'll pay you your deposit. Can I do that right now with a card?'

'Of course, Mrs Pargeter. And I should warn you that if you were to cancel within three weeks of the booked date, you would be liable for paying the full costs of our services. And because of the late booking, that three weeks is approaching rather soon.'

'Fine,' said Mrs Pargeter blithely. 'And once I've paid, I'd like to fix up a date when the bride, whose name's Samantha Pinkerton, and her fiancé, who's Kelvin but I don't know his surname, can come along and check out the premises.'

The very substantial deposit was made on Mrs Pargeter's card, and a visit for Sammy and Kelvin was provisionally arranged for the following Monday. Mrs Pargeter agreed that she would check that the two young people would be free then and only ring back if the date had to be changed.

Then, as she was about to say her goodbyes, Shereen interrupted. 'Oh, there is one other thing . . .'

'Yes?'

'The couple who were going to be married on the twenty-seventh of May were going to use the chapel and have a religious service.'

'Very nice too.'

'So I don't know whether Samantha and Kelvin would like to do the same?'

'They would.'

'Good. That means I don't have to cancel the vicar.'

'Oh, yes, you do,' said Mrs Pargeter. 'Stand him down. We'll be bringing our own vicar.'

St-Crispin-in-the-Closet is one of the lesser known churches in the City of London and also one of the few medieval structures to have survived the Great Fire. A narrow building, it is squashed between tall corporate edifices in a little alley off Lace Bobbin Street, like a pocket bible on a shelf between atlases.

Gary's Bentley didn't look so conspicuous in the City that afternoon. There were a lot of them around. Also, as if neatly to point out the downside of consumerism, a scruffy man with a scruffy dog sat on the pavement at the corner of Lace Bobbin Street hawking *The Big Issue*. He didn't look particularly enamoured of his task, but sales of the magazine were hopefully helping to get him off the streets.

As Gary opened the car's back door outside the church's round-topped Norman archway, he asked, as ever, 'Come with you or stay, Mrs P?'

'Stay – or go off and do something else for an hour. I don't want to frighten him by being with someone he might recognize from the old days.'

'Right you are.' Gary's eyes followed her generous figure as she handed twenty pounds to the *Big Issue* seller and refused the magazine. Continuing to watch as Mrs Pargeter entered a small door inset into the two large ones, Gary realized once again why all of his relationships ended in disaster. His heart was committed elsewhere. None of the girls who were so willing to go to bed with him could match up to Mrs Pargeter.

Inside the church a short chubby man in a cassock was at the altar replacing burnt-down candles in the candlesticks with new ones. The top of his head was bald, but encircled by an almost monastic horseshoe shape of long grey hair. He looked up nervously at the sound of the opening door, but his brow cleared when he saw who the new arrival was. (Mrs Pargeter had taken the precaution of a preliminary phone call.)

'My dear creature!' he said, bustling up the aisle to throw his arms around her. 'How wonderful to see you!'

'You too, Holy.' It was perhaps inevitable that someone called the Rev. Smirke should be known to Mr Pargeter's associates as 'Holy' Smirke.

'Sad to think we haven't met since I conducted your dear husband's funeral.'

'It was a sad occasion, yes, but you did it beautifully.'

'I had a lot of help from so many people. Truffler Mason guarding the main doors, dear Gary providing the getaway cars . . .'

'The hearse and funeral cars, Holy,' she gently corrected him.

'Yes, of course, that's what I meant.'

She looked round the church. 'Lovely place. You seem very settled in here.'

'Oh yes, Mrs Pargeter. A case of the prodigal having returned. I'm up to here with fatted calf, you know. I'm in charge of one of the most beautiful churches in the City of London – or anywhere else, come to that.'

Mrs Pargeter took in her surroundings. Tall arching columns, stone monuments, a floor paved black and white, darkly gleaming wood, shiny brass, and the whole subtly lit by the colours from the stained glass windows. A celebration of all that was beautiful. Mankind bringing the best of its skills to the celebration of the Almighty. Though not a believer herself, Mrs Pargeter understood how surroundings like these could foster faith in the most cynical of hearts.

'And are you settled domestically as well?' Mrs Pargeter recalled that the Rev. Smirke, in spite of his unprepossessing appearance, had had a surprisingly varied emotional life.

'Oh yes, thank you. There is a very nice little flat just behind the church. And I have a housekeeper. A *French* housekeeper,' he added with relish.

She looked at him quizzically. 'Is that a "housekeeper" in the sense that some Catholic priests have "housekeepers"?'

'Oh yes,' he replied roguishly. 'Except, of course, because I'm an Anglican, for me there's no sin involved.'

'Isn't there something in the Bible about not having sex outside marriage?'

'Oh, I don't think it's put quite like that. And it's not one of the important bits. There's lots of stuff in the Bible that God didn't really mean.'

'I see. And who is the judge of which bits God did mean and which he didn't?'

'Well, I am, obviously. I am his priest, his representative on earth.'

'You've got it all worked out.'

'I certainly have.'

'Very satisfactory.'

He reached into his cassock and produced a card, which he passed to her. 'That's the office number and the flat. If a woman answers—'

'A woman with a French accent?'

'Yes. Her name's Ernestine.'

'Fine,' said Mrs Pargeter.

'Anyway, take a pew.' Holy Smirke chuckled. 'I do love saying that in church. People use the expression so often, but so rarely in the right context. And then, of course, there's the old schoolboy joke which never fails to tickle me: "He who farts in church must sit in his own pew!"'

Another loud chuckle, in which Mrs Pargeter joined. 'I see you haven't lost your sense of humour, Holy.'

'Heaven forfend that any of us should ever lose our sense of humour, Mrs Pargeter. Where would we be without it?'

'Do you think God has a sense of humour?'

'Of course he does. It's evident wherever you look in all of his creation. Don't try telling me that the power which contrived to create the duck-billed platypus didn't have a sense of humour. Then again, how else do you explain the politicians God has put in place to rule over us . . . not to mention many of the people he has chosen to become television presenters? But enough of this idle badinage. You are here on professional business, Mrs Pargeter. Of which of my many services –' he chuckled again – 'and I use the word advisedly – do you wish to take advantage?'

'I want you to officiate at a wedding.'

'What kind of wedding?'

'Well, an ordinary church wedding.'

'No, Mrs Pargeter, I meant: is this a legal wedding? Will the young couple have met before the day of the ceremony? Will they see each other again after the ceremony? Or is it a sham? Is the event set up merely to cement the immigration status of one or other of them?'

'It is a completely legal wedding!' said Mrs Pargeter with some vehemence. 'I thought you'd put all that other stuff behind you, Holy.'

'I am so sorry, Mrs Pargeter,' he said shamefacedly. 'Old habits die hard.'

'So long as they die, that's all that concerns me.'

'Oh, they do. They do die. They are long dead. I haven't offended against either the criminal code or the moral code since . . . ooh, let me think.'

'When was it? A very long time ago, I hope.'

He coloured. 'I'm afraid I have to confess that it was last Sunday. The Devil tempted me to trouser a twenty-pound note from the collection.'

'Holy!'

'Oh, the Devil can be very persuasive, you know. Even Our Lord found him a fairly tricky customer in the wilderness. Besides, it is so rare that we get a twenty-pound note in the collection bag. I felt I really had to keep it for its souvenir value.'

'That doesn't wash with me, Holy. You see that that twenty pounds is returned to the collection next Sunday!'

'Mrs Pargeter, you are a hard taskmistress.'

'Are you going to return it?' She could be quite scary when she was in this mode.

'Well, I—'

'Or do you think God's got such a good sense of humour that he'll regard you keeping the money as a huge joke?'

'I have always believed in a benevolent God.'

'So benevolent that he would condone robbery?'

'Well, yes. I have thought this through, you know. I've even written a sermon on the subject.'

'The subject of God approving of robbery?'

'Yes.'

'Have you delivered it yet?'

'No, I'm waiting for the right moment.'

'You might have a long wait. So what's your argument?'

'Well, it's all based on scriptural fact. And most of it comes from Jesus the Son rather than God the Father.'

'OK. Go on.'

'Now, you'll agree with me that Jesus Christ, as tradition-ally represented, is not acquisitive and is very forgiving?'

'I'll give you that, yes.'

'So if I were to steal something from him, it wouldn't matter to him, because he's not acquisitive. And because he has a forgiving nature, he'd forgive me . . .'

'Ye-es,' said Mrs Pargeter cautiously, concentrating on the argument.

'So Jesus isn't hurt by the theft . . .'

'No.'

'. . . which means it's a victimless crime.' Mrs Pargeter was too gobsmacked to say anything as Holy Smirke continued: 'Now, there's an instance in the Bible where Jesus shows that he's on the side of thieves.'

'I very much doubt that, Holy.'

'Oh, there is. It's mentioned in all four gospels. Sometimes called "The Cleansing of the Temple".'

'When he threw out the moneylenders?'

'Exactly. And in Matthew he says the moneylenders have turned the temple into a "den of thieves".'

'But he doesn't say that with any sense of approval.'

Holy Smirke held up his hand. 'If you would let me finish, Mrs Pargeter. Now, what's the other thing Jesus does in the temple? He overturns the tables of the moneylenders. And what is on these tables? Money, of course – they're money-lenders, aren't they? So if you overturn a moneylenders' table – and remember they didn't have notes in those days – all the coins are going to go rolling all over the floor, aren't they? And you get coins rolling all over the floor in a den of thieves – what's going to happen? Obviously, the thieves are going to pocket as many of the coins as they can. Which means –' the clergyman spread his hands wide, as if his thesis had just been proved – 'that Jesus not only approved of thieves, he actually acted as their accomplice.'

There was quite a long silence before Mrs Pargeter said, 'You didn't train as a Jesuit, did you, Holy?'

'No.'

'Well, I still think I'd leave it a while before you deliver that sermon.'

'But you can't fault its logic, can you?'

'Well, I think there might be one or two minor flaws in there, actually.'

'Oh.' Holy Smirke sounded genuinely disappointed. 'As I say, I believe in a benevolent God, and I'm sure it would be in his nature to overlook the minor peccadillos of some of his less scrupulous—'

'That's not the point, Holy. What I want to know is: are you going to return that twenty pounds you took from last Sunday's collection?'

He crumbled instantly. 'Yes, of course, Mrs Pargeter.'

'Good.' She was glad to be moving on from religious exegesis to more practical matters. 'Now, the date of the wedding for which your services are required is the twenty-seventh of May.'

'What day of the week is that?'

'It's a Saturday.'

'Oh, that should be all right. I tend to have certain commitments on Sundays, but otherwise my time's my own.'

'I thought your time was God's.'

'Yes, well, we kind of share it. A celestial timeshare.'

'Hm.' Mrs Pargeter focused her violet eyes on Holy Smirke's face. 'So, have you really gone straight?'

'Oh, I like to think so.'

'I'm sure you like to think so – I'd like to think so too – but that doesn't really answer my question.' She repeated it, lest there be any uncertainty about what she meant. 'Have you really gone straight?'

'Well, up to a point,' was the best answer he could supply.

Mrs Pargeter shook her head with frustration. 'My husband worked very hard to look after all the people who worked for him.'

'Yes, I know. I—'

'Quiet, I haven't finished! And before he died he offered training and job opportunities to all of his staff, so that they could make their legitimate way forward in life.'

'But I—'

'My husband paid for you to go to theological college so that you could become properly ordained. He changed you from someone who wore a dog collar so that people wouldn't suspect him to the genuine article. Are you not grateful for what he did for you?'

'Yes, of course, I'm extremely grateful, but—'

'I know. Old habits die hard; you've already told me that.'

'I mean, Mrs Pargeter, in no way am I now a professional criminal . . .'

'I am glad to hear that.'

'. . . but I do like to dabble a bit on the side. You know, in a strictly amateur way.'

'Like it's a hobby?'

'Exactly. That's a very good way of putting it.'

'Well, get another hobby!' said Mrs Pargeter with a firmness that could not be denied.

'Yes, of course, immediately,' he hastened to assure her. Then he looked dubious. 'I wonder if I'd be any good at macramé . . .'

'Anyway, I must go.' She took out her mobile and texted Gary so that he would have the Bentley outside waiting.

'Yes, of course.' Holy Smirke sighed nostalgically. 'Oh, I keep thinking back to the wonderful times we had when I was working for your husband. I miss him.'

'So,' said Mrs Pargeter with a wry grin, 'do I.'

'Of course, of course you would. I suppose what I mean is that I miss the excitement of the very early days, you know, when we were involved in setting up a brand-new enterprise. It was seat-of-the-pants thrilling, and your husband was such a brilliant organizer. I knew that I was in at the start of something that was going to be monumentally successful. And so, of course, it proved.'

Mrs Pargeter nodded fondly, proud of her husband's great achievements. Then a thought struck her. 'Holy, you said you were in with my husband right from the start?'

'Absolutely. Founder member.' As he reminisced, his vicarly tones gave way to something more East End and earthy. 'We was at school together. That's where it all started.'

'So,' asked Mrs Pargeter, 'did you know someone called Normington Winthrop?'

NINE

B efore she could ask any more questions there was the sound of the small door at the front of the church opening. Holy Smirke looked up and checked his watch. 'Oh dear, I'd forgotten. I have a four o'clock appointment. Woman coming to talk about arrangements for her husband's funeral. I'm afraid she's a stickler for detail,' he whispered. 'Could take some time.'

'Don't worry, I'll give you a call. Are you in this evening?'

'Oh yes,' he said with relish. 'Ernestine's cooking *cassoulet*.'

'Very nice too. I'll call you . . . what, round nine?'

'That would be perfect. By then the *cassoulet* will be sitting lightly on my stomach and I'll be enjoying a *digestif*.'

'Excellent.'

The two women exchanged discreet nods, and as she made her way to the exit Mrs Pargeter heard a very fulsome Holy Smirke say, 'My dear lady, I was so sorry to hear of your loss.'

'No loss to me,' the woman replied with frosted Kensington vowels. 'I'm just glad to be shot of the old git.'

Safely delivered back home by Gary in the Bentley, Mrs Pargeter looked vaguely into her kitchen but didn't even get as far as opening the fridge. She wouldn't cook that evening. When the time came she'd phone for a takeaway from her favourite local Indian.

While she was sitting with a gin and tonic waiting for supper, idly flipping through a bridal magazine (she'd stocked up with a lot of them so that she could keep up to speed with Sammy), she had a phone call from Erin Jarvis.

'Anything to report?' Mrs Pargeter asked eagerly.

'Well, first of all I've got the information about Passport Pinkerton that his daughter wanted.'

'Oh, she'll be delighted with that. I gave her your number, didn't I?'

'Yes, you did. I've spoken to her, and she's over the moon about it. We're meeting up for coffee tomorrow to talk it through.'

'Great. You'll love Sammy; she's a terrific girl.' But both of them knew that this was not the most important part of their conversation. 'So,' said Mrs Pargeter. 'Did you find anything in the physical archive about Normington Winthrop?'

'Well, it's interesting,' said the girl. 'It's not so much what's in the archive as what *isn't* in the archive.'

'The dog that didn't bark in the night-time?'

'Exactly. As you know, your husband was a meticulous record-keeper.'

'Meticulous in everything he did,' said Mrs Pargeter fondly.

'And in his records of his early . . . er, business ventures he gives credit where appropriate to every one of his associates . . . except, of course, the one whose name has been so carefully excised from the notebooks.'

'Normington Winthrop,' said Mrs Pargeter excitedly.

'We don't know for sure that it's him, but that's a possibility. Anyway, whoever tampered with the notebooks was clearly given instruction to cut out the name, which he or she has done with punctilious efficiency. But there are one or two references to another associate which haven't been cut out.'

'And why do you think that is?'

'It's because, Mrs Pargeter, the references to him are not made by name. He's given a kind of nickname, and clearly the saboteur with his pair of scissors wasn't told to look out for that.'

'So what is the nickname?'

'"The Armourer",' said Erin Jarvis.

Mrs Pargeter had finished her delicious Indian banquet. Having relished every mouthful of her prawn puri and chicken dhansak and swept up the residual juices with naan bread, she was about to return to reading a pivotal debate on the optimum size of a bride's bouquet when she noticed the time. Just after nine.

She rang the number on Holy Smirke's card and, as promised, the answer had a French accent. A lovely, very warm, sensual French accent. Holy had certainly landed on his feet when Ernestine was appointed as his housekeeper.

'Could I speak to . . .' Mrs Pargeter suddenly realized that his nickname might not be in general usage and continued: 'The Reverend Smirke?'

'I am sorry. That, I am afraid, you cannot do. Holy is not here.'

So at least Ernestine used it. Mrs Pargeter wondered if his parishioners did too. 'Oh. He said he would be in if I rang at nine.'

'Who am I speaking to?'

'My name is Mrs Pargeter.'

'Ah.' The woman sounded relieved. 'Holy has mentioned you. He holds you in very high regard.'

'I'm honoured.'

'Also, he always speaks very highly of your husband. He it was, I believe, who paid for Holy's training for the priesthood?'

'Yes, that's right.'

'He was a very generous man, I think.'

'Yes, very generous.' Mrs Pargeter couldn't prevent her eyes from moving towards the photograph of her dark-suited husband on the mantelpiece.

'Anyway, I am sorry, Mrs Pargeter, that Holy is not here to speak to you.'

'Have you any idea when he will be back?'

'No, not at all.' For the first time there was an edge of anxiety in the woman's voice. 'Normally, on weekdays he comes back to the flat at six thirty on the dot. But today, no.'

'Maybe he had an urgent call from one of his parishioners?'

'I do not think so. He is always very good about telling me where he is going. He calls me on the mobile. And it is very unlike him to be late for a meal.'

'Particularly, I gather, when you are cooking *cassoulet*.'

'Ah, he told you, yes. It is indeed one of his favourite dishes.' Ernestine sounded almost on the verge of tears. 'It is unlike Holy to miss his *cassoulet*.' She caressed the word, as if it were symbolic of some more intimate treat.

'I'm sure he'll be fine,' said Mrs Pargeter, sounding more confident than she felt. 'Just got held up somewhere.'

'Yes. Perhaps. I hope.' But Ernestine didn't sound convinced.

'Well, look, I'll be up till ten thirty, so if he's in before that, could you ask him to give me a call?'

'Yes, of course.' Once again emotion threatened to overwhelm her. 'But if Holy does not come back . . .? If he is not here in the morning . . .?'

'Ring me,' said Mrs Pargeter firmly.

It was half-past seven the following morning when the phone on Mrs Pargeter's bedside table rang. It was Ernestine.

'I am sorry it is so early. I have been awake all night. Holy has not come home.'

TEN

Mrs Pargeter instantly rang Truffler Mason and agreed to meet him at eleven outside St-Crispin-in-the-Closet. She texted Gary, and he was at her house within twenty minutes.

'I haven't had an invoice from you for months,' said Mrs Pargeter once she was settled into the back of the car. 'And you've done a hell of a lot of driving for me recently.'

'I'm on the case,' Gary lied.

Truffler Mason was outside the church as agreed, his expression again that of a man whose investments had all just vanished in a major financial crash. 'Good morning, Mrs Pargeter,' he said lugubriously. 'Wonderful to see you, as ever.'

'Am I coming with you this time?' asked Gary.

'Yes, please. Will the car be all right here?' The Bentley had been drawn up half on the pavement, straddling the double yellow lines.

Gary reached inside the glove compartment and took out a rolled-up small flag on a stick. As he affixed it to the front of the Bentley's roof, the fabric unfurled to reveal that it was the Royal Standard. 'Usually works,' said Gary.

Ernestine looked as warm and sexy as her voice had promised. Her hair was dyed a rich brown and cut stylishly short. Probably over seventy, she had that Frenchwoman's knack of looking elegant in any circumstances, even those as unhappy as her current situation.

She served excellent coffee in the tiny but snug flat behind the church and told them what she could about Holy Smirke's disappearance. Which wasn't very much, really. He just hadn't returned to the flat; that was all there was to it.

'Have you looked in the church?' asked Mrs Pargeter.

'Of course I have. One of my first thoughts was that he might have had a fall – or perhaps worse, a stroke – but there was no sign of him anywhere.'

'And no signs of a struggle?' asked Truffler. 'No evidence that anyone else had been in the church?'

'No.'

'Because I was trying to think what time I left him yesterday,' Mrs Pargeter mused. 'Oh yes, it was just on four because Holy had a four o'clock appointment with a woman about her husband's funeral arrangements. I wonder if we could track her down, find out when she left him and whether she witnessed anything unusual.'

'I have spoken to her,' said Ernestine.

'Oh?'

'Her name was in the church diary. With her phone number. So I telephone her this morning. She tells me she leave soon after five. Holy stays in the church. He does not say anything to her about going out.'

'She could be lying, I suppose,' said Gary.

'Yes, but we really have no reason to be suspicious of her.'

'No, Mrs P,' Truffler agreed. 'Just the circumstantial fact that she may have been the last person to see Holy before he disappeared.'

Mrs Pargeter turned the beam of her violet eyes on to Ernestine. 'So there was nothing at all that seemed unusual when you searched the church?'

'Well, there was one thing . . .'

'Something missing?'

'No. More the other way around. There was something there that I would not have expected to be there.'

'Oh?'

'You know that Holy does not have a lot of hair on top of his head . . .?'

'You can't help noticing that.'

'And he feels the cold very much. Even when the weather gets warmer, he never goes out without his . . . what do you call it? "Flat hat"?'

'"Flat cap", maybe?'

'Yes, this is good. This is what he calls it. Well, it is there, the flat cap. It is still hanging on the hook in the vestry where he always puts it.'

'Which means?'

'Holy did not mean to go out. If he intended to go outside he would definitely have worn his flat cap.'

'So,' said Mrs Pargeter, 'we might conclude from that that someone forced him to leave the church.'

Truffler Mason and Gary made a very full examination of the interior of St-Crispin-in-the-Closet, looking for any clues as to the circumstances of Holy Smirke's departure from the church the previous afternoon. They found nothing.

While the two men were doing their search, Mrs Pargeter drank more coffee with Ernestine, giving her constant reassurances that Holy Smirke would be found, that she had at her disposal the finest team of investigators in the country. She then asked rather tentatively if Ernestine had thought of calling the police. The Frenchwoman said no, Holy had always wanted to have as little as possible to do with the police. Mrs Pargeter was with him on that.

It was only when she had said her goodbyes and was about to enter the Bentley (the Royal Standard, having saved it from the ministrations of traffic wardens, had now been stowed away) that she stopped suddenly and said, '*Big Issue.*'

Truffler Mason looked perplexed. 'Do you want me to buy you one? Or are you selling them?'

'No, no. There was a man on the corner selling them yesterday. He was sitting on the pavement just here with a dog. He might have witnessed something.'

'I remember him,' said Gary, then, stating the obvious, continued, 'but he's not here today.'

'He might have just shifted his pitch. Drive along Lace Bobbin Street and see if you can spot him.'

It was a shrewd suggestion. Less than a hundred yards away the scruffy man with the scruffy dog was sitting hopefully on the pavement with his stock of magazines. He recognized the Bentley and rose to his feet. He also recognized Mrs Pargeter. Not many of his customers gave him twenty pounds and didn't even take a copy of the magazine.

When asked about the comings and goings at St-Crispin-in-the-Closet the previous afternoon, he proved to be a very observant witness.

'It was early evening yesterday. I remember because I was thinking of packing it in for the day. Evening rush hour is hopeless for my business. Everyone too keen to get home, scurrying off for their buses and tubes. If they want something to read on the journey, they pick up an *Evening Standard*, because that's free, apart from anything else. They certainly don't stop for a *Big Issue*. Mornings are a bit better, but—'

Mrs Pargeter raised a hand to stop his flow. 'Sorry, what did you see early evening yesterday? Did you see a clergyman in a cassock come out of St-Crispin-in-the-Closet?'

'Certainly did. One of those Toyota Priuses – you know, hybrid cars – parked just at the end of the lane, where you parked yesterday and all. Two men got out and went into the church. Couple of minutes later out they come, with the vicar in tow.'

'Did he appear to be coming with them willingly?'

'Yes. Well, he did at first.'

'How d'you mean?'

'They get to the car, and one of the men – big guy he was, must've spent a lot of time in the gym – he says, "It's really urgent. There's this bloke who's dying, needs to have his last rites," and the clergyman says, "Last rites are a Catholic sacrament, and I'm Church of England." And the big guy says, "Never mind that," opens the back door of the Prius and shoves the vicar in. Smaller guy leaps into the driver's seat, and they screech off like they got all the hounds of hell after them.'

'So you reckon the vicar was kidnapped?'

'Looked like it, yeah.'

They asked further questions, but the *Big Issue* seller had little more information to give. He hadn't taken note of the Prius's number plate. He wasn't sure if he'd recognize the two men again. All he could tell them was that the car had gone off on the road out of the City in the direction of South London.

After their encounter with the witness they all felt rather flat. Gary suggested he drive Mrs Pargeter back to Essex and drop Truffler by a tube station so that he could return to his office.

'But we must find Holy,' said Mrs Pargeter.

'Sure. We'll do our best.' Truffler didn't sound very hopeful. Mind you, he never actually sounded very hopeful.

'I thought you were something of an expert on Missing Persons.'

'I've had a few successes,' Truffler admitted, 'but I've always had a bit more to go on than we've got here.'

'Hm.' Mrs Pargeter took the little black book out of her handbag and flicked through the entries. 'My husband entered you in here with your specialism listed as "Missing Persons".'

'Generous of him, but, as I say, my track record isn't that great.'

'Are there any other names in there under "Missing Persons"?' asked Gary.

Mrs Pargeter checked the relevant entries. Quite a few names had been scored through with a single neat blue line from her husband's italic fountain pen. She had worked out that these represented people who had passed on to that great Investigative Bureau in the Sky.

'Just one,' she replied. '"Napper" Johnson.'

Both men immediately let out a whoop of joy. Even Truffler Mason sounded mildly cheerful.

'Napper Johnson!' he said. 'Now you're talking!'

ELEVEN

Erin Jarvis and Sammy Pinkerton met up in a nice (i.e. not part of a chain) coffee shop in Covent Garden on Thursday afternoon. There was an instant rapport between the two, and almost immediately – in the way women always can and men very rarely can – they were talking with deep emotion. Both had recently lost their fathers, and though Erin was further down the road of coming to terms with the fact, they had a lot of common experience to talk about.

So they had shared many secrets by the time they got on to the real purpose of their meeting. After getting in their second round of coffees, Erin handed Sammy a cardboard folder. 'This is all the stuff I could find on your father.'

Sammy opened the folder to reveal a pile of printed sheets the thickness of a short novel. 'Wow,' she said, 'that's awesome!'

'I'm not expecting you to read it straight away,' said Erin, flicking back her purple hair. 'But when you do get into it, if there's anything you want developed or amplified just give me a call.'

Then they got on to the topic of Sammy's forthcoming wedding, and Kelvin, and the general inadequacies of boyfriends. Erin had had quite a roller coaster of an emotional history and was currently enjoying being unattached. 'The trouble is I'm really a workaholic, and it's sometimes difficult for blokes to take that on board.'

'Yes, Kelvin's very caught up in his work. I sometimes think it's the only thing he's interested in,' Sammy agreed ruefully. But she didn't specify what that work was.

When the two girls parted, they realized that they had been there for over two hours, and they had formed a very strong bond.

Sammy Pinkerton's last words to her new friend were: 'You must come to my hen party on Saturday. I'll email you the details.'

*   *   *

Their appointment with Napper Johnson – or, as he was now known, Victor Johnson of Johnson Caterham Consultants – was at his Canary Wharf offices. They were to see him as soon as they arrived, no matter the time. 'Everything else out of the diary for Mrs Pargeter,' he'd said when Mrs Pargeter rang him earlier that day from the Bentley, after speaking to the *Big Issue* seller. 'When I think of all the things your late husband did for me . . .'

After a good fish and chips lunch, as the Bentley probed its way through the East End traffic, Truffler and Gary reminisced fondly about the exploits of the legend they were about to visit.

'Remember, Gary, what Napper did with those two security guards on the Fulham safe-deposit job? Only flew them off on a package holiday to Torremolinos! End of the fortnight they were having such a good time they didn't want to come back.'

'I think the reason they didn't want to come back was more the reaction they were likely to get from their boss when he found the safes had been cleaned out.'

'You're probably right, Gary.'

'Then do you remember what Napper done with those two Arab princesses? Kept them locked in a suite at Claridges – only the same blooming hotel where their dad the Sultan was staying – and where he received the ransom demand. And he knew nothing about it till he'd agreed to fly back the two of Mr P's men who'd been arrested for the jewellery scam out in his country . . . Can't remember where it was. One of the United Arab Emirates, anyway.'

'Then there was the time Napper nicked that—'

'I can't help observing,' Mrs Pargeter interposed rather coldly, 'that the cases you refer to seem to involve your colleague actually *kidnapping* people rather than finding and releasing those who have *been* kidnapped.'

Rather embarrassedly, remembering whose company they were in, Truffler and Gary fell over themselves to assure Mrs Pargeter that Napper Johnson had performed a lot of the other kind of service as well.

*   *   *

The man himself was suave almost to the point – but not quite – of being oleaginous. So much so that Mrs Pargeter's first reaction was one of suspicion. She had met enough smoothies in her time to distrust the breed, and although Napper Johnson had the endorsement of Truffler and Gary – and had, indeed, worked for her late husband – there was something about him she didn't warm to. The charm he exuded didn't seem quite authentic.

The grey hair above his chubby face was cut with a stylish quiff, and his three-piece blue suit had been elegantly tailored to accommodate a growing midriff. The office behind the massive desk at which he sat commanded an extensive view of the Thames snaking its way between the ancient monuments and lesser buildings of London's financial district.

When introductions had been made and coffee ordered, Mrs Pargeter, with characteristic, but nonetheless charming, bluntness, asked, 'So, what does "Consultants" mean?'

'As in "Johnson Caterham Consultants"?'

'Exactly.'

He smiled.

'Could cover a multitude of sins, that,' she said.

He smiled again. 'I'm sure it could. And I'm sure it has – particularly in the City of London. Though I would like to point out that all businesses on which I now consult are entirely legitimate.'

Mrs Pargeter grinned. 'That's what they all say.'

Napper Johnson grinned back. He was clearly enjoying this exchange of banter. There had already developed a mutual respect for the other's intelligence. But there was still an element of caution on Mrs Pargeter's side and an element of world-weariness on his.

'So, are you still involved in kidnapping?'

He winced at her use of the word. 'I would prefer to describe the scope of my activities as covering the world of public relations.'

'Oh, really? So when a member of the public wants one of their relations to disappear for a while, then you're on hand to make the arrangements?'

'Again, those are not the words I would use, Mrs Pargeter.

But a lot of the business of public relations does involve the keeping apart of potentially combustible combinations of people. So if I get requests to make such arrangements, I am more than happy to comply with them.'

'And in what kind of circumstances might such requests be made?'

Napper Johnson spread his hands to indicate the wide variety of scenarios that might call for his services. 'A lot of it is family stuff. Let us say, if it might be thought preferable that a divorced father should not be available to attend his daughter's wedding, that could be arranged. Loving parents might prefer that an unsuitable boyfriend should spend the next year in South America. An inconvenient mother-in-law could perhaps stay on the Costa Brava for a few months. Those are the kind of arrangements my company is happy to make.'

'But no charges of kidnapping or abduction ever ensue?'

He looked pained by the suggestion. 'Of course not, Mrs Pargeter. We are far too careful in our business management to let such a situation occur.'

'I see.'

Truffler Mason and Gary had been watching this exchange with some anxiety. Having made the introduction to Napper Johnson, they were worried to hear their patron apparently looking this gift horse in the mouth. They were also a little worried by the way the consultant appeared almost to be on autopilot rather than deeply engaged in their problem.

'But you have done some kind of charitable jobs too, haven't you, Napper?' said Truffler. 'Helping people who needed to do a vanishing act. Lord Lucan was one of yours, wasn't he?'

'And Shergar,' Gary contributed.

These, however, were not examples on which the consultant wished to dwell. 'Both a long time ago,' he said dismissively. 'And both – as I subsequently discovered, though of course didn't know at the time – cases which had some degree of criminal connection. Now, as I say, Mrs Pargeter, I am much more selective in the clients I take on.'

'Hm.' She still didn't sound completely convinced.

Truffler continued trying to ease the process. 'In fact,

Napper,' he said, 'it was more the other side of your business that Mrs Pargeter was interested in.'

'Oh?'

Gary spelled it out. 'There's someone she knows who's been kidnapped, and she wants to find him. Isn't that right, Mrs P?'

She admitted that what he had asserted was indeed the case, and Napper Johnson's chubby face was instantly wreathed in smiles. 'Ah, if only you had said that straight away, Mrs Pargeter. That is the aspect of Napper Caterham Consultants which we have been developing enormously in recent years. And I have no hesitation in stating that our record in the finding and release of kidnap victims is now second to none.'

'Congratulations,' said Mrs Pargeter drily, still not totally convinced, still waiting for more.

'We do make certain restrictions for obvious reasons. We don't involve ourselves in international politics, so if the kidnap victim were, let us say, in the Middle East, my company would not be the right service to call on. But anything within this country, so long as it has no terrorism connection, is very much our kind of business. So who, may I ask, Mrs Pargeter, is the individual whose release you wish to effect?'

'He was yet another person who worked with my husband – who was with him right from the start of his operations, in fact. Have you heard of someone called Holy Smirke?'

'Indeed I have, Mrs Pargeter. And I've heard nothing but good of him. Though, sadly, I've never had the pleasure of meeting the gentleman in question, I know him to have been one of your late husband's first associates. I believe the two of them were actually at school together.'

This thorough knowledge of Holy Smirke's background finally convinced Mrs Pargeter that she was dealing with someone she could trust. She beamed as she said, 'You're absolutely right.'

'And I am so sorry to hear that the Reverend Smirke has been kidnapped. Could you tell me as much as you know of the circumstances of his abduction?'

This Mrs Pargeter, with interpolations from Truffler and Gary, quickly provided.

When they had finished, Napper Johnson linked his hands

over his well-rounded stomach and smiled beatifically. 'Well, that shouldn't be too much trouble,' he said. 'We've solved many cases where we have had considerably less information. To know the exact site where the abduction took place is an enormous bonus.'

'So how do you proceed from here?' asked Mrs Pargeter. 'Or is that a professional secret?'

'It is indeed a professional secret, and one that I would not willingly divulge to anyone . . .' He smiled. 'Except, of course, to you, Mrs Pargeter.'

She was now completely charmed by Napper Johnson and wondered why she had ever doubted his integrity. 'So how's it done?' she asked.

'Well, there are a variety of methods we use, depending on the circumstances. In these offices I have experts in many forms of information-gathering and, as with many businesses, information is the key to our operation. In this instance we are extraordinarily fortunate that the abduction took place in a busy urban environment.'

'Oh, really? Why? More witnesses?'

'Well, in this case, thanks to your vigilance, Mrs Pargeter, we do in fact have a witness in the form of the *Big Issue* seller. But, more important than that, we have CCTV.'

'You mean you have your own CCTV?'

'Good heavens, no, Mrs Pargeter. I don't have to go to the expense of having my own. The Metropolitan and City police are generous enough to provide that service for me.'

'How d'you mean?'

'I have amongst the experts on my staff people who are capable of accessing all the information recorded on the police CCTV systems.'

'You mean, like, *hacking*?'

'*Accessing* is the word I prefer, Mrs Pargeter.'

'Very well.'

'Perhaps I could give you a demonstration? Remind me of the precise location and the approximate timing of Holy Smirke's abduction.'

Mrs Pargeter provided the relevant details. Napper Johnson pressed down a button on his intercom and relayed the information to some unseen minion. Then he swung the large screen on his desk round so that it faced his three visitors. 'Shouldn't take long,' he said.

And within seconds the screen filled with a view from the roadside end of the alley into which St-Crispin-in-the-Closet was crammed. A Toyota Prius was parked in the forefront of the image. The small door in the church's large doors opened to reveal Holy Smirke being escorted out by two men. Their conversation, which could not be heard, appeared to be affable. It was only when they were close to the car that the atmosphere changed. While the shorter of the abductors rushed round to get in the driving seat, the larger forced the unfortunate vicar into the back seat. The moment his door was closed, the Prius sped off out of the City.

It was then that the unseen operator of the video process showed his or her skill. The camera focused on the back of the car and enlarged the image to give a very clear reading of its number plate. He or she then produced close-up still photographs of the two abductors.

'Won't take us long to identify them from our database,' said Napper with a note of justifiable smugness.

Then, for good measure, the camera homed in on the *Big Issue* seller.

'And there, of course, is your witness.' Napper Johnson smiled one of his smoothest smiles. 'I don't think it should take us too long to sort out this little job for you, Mrs Pargeter.'

'Napper's good,' said Gary as they drove away from Canary Wharf.

'Yes,' Truffler agreed, 'but you didn't take to him straight away, did you, Mrs P?'

'Very observant of you. No, there was something I kind of distrusted at first. In spite of all the obvious bonhomie, he seemed rather distant, as though he was just going through the motions.'

'Yes, I noticed that.' Gary nodded. 'He's still got all the *spiel*, but he didn't have that enthusiasm for the work he always used to have. Maybe he's just getting old and tired.'

'No, there's more to it than that,' said Truffler. 'I heard from someone that his wife died a couple of years back. Lovely woman, apparently. And though Napper's working as much as ever, nothing's felt the same for him since he lost her.'

'Well, I understand that feeling,' said Mrs Pargeter.

TWELVE

'Look, you don't have to tell me about caring for a father,' said Sammy Pinkerton. 'I spent nearly three years looking after mine, remember.'

'I know,' said her fiancé. 'And I wish I'd had the opportunity to do the same for my old man.'

'We've been through all this before,' said Sammy disconsolately.

They made an attractive couple, the girl's almost exotically dark colouring in marked contrast to the boy's blue eyes and Nordic pale hair. His body was long and thin. They were sitting in the Greyhound, a pub just round the corner from their flat in Southend, on Thursday evening. It had been the scene of many happy occasions between them over the months of their relationship, but now what it witnessed more frequently were arguments. And almost always about the same thing.

Kelvin Stockett's angular body was hunched into his chair, full of unloaded aggression. 'I blame my mother,' he said. 'She deliberately kept me apart from my dad.'

'And always made you refer to him as Daddy. I *know*,' she said with a sigh. She was aware that when her fiancé was in this mood he would just go round and round in the same mournful circles.

'She deliberately stopped me from having any kind of relationship with him.'

'I know, but she was doing the right thing, according to her principles.'

'Her principles were nothing more than snobbery. And the situation wasn't helped by the fact that her father had been a Chief Constable, and she kind of hero-worshipped him. From the moment she got hitched to my old man, she was convinced she had married beneath herself. That's why she had my birth registered under her surname rather than his. I should have been called Kelvin Mitchell. My mother was, like, disowning her own husband. And she regarded all the money he brought into the house, the means whereby she was able to live such a comfortable life, as somehow tainted.'

Sammy Pinkerton waited for the attack that would inevitably follow. Sure enough, Kelvin said, 'Just in the same way that you regard my money.'

'I've told you many times, Kelvin. It's a matter of principle for me. I won't accept money that's been got by burglary.'

'But you know why I'm a burglar, don't you?'

'Yes, yes, yes. You've told me a million times. You do it out of respect for your father.'

'Exactly. I wasn't allowed to have a relationship with him while he was alive; I wasn't allowed to show pride in his achievements. I wasn't even allowed to know what those achievements were. My mother kept all that from me. And now I'm trying to repair that terrible breach of faith. I am showing respect for what my father stood for.'

'What he stood for led to him standing up in courtrooms, on more than one occasion, and being sent away to prison.'

'I know.'

Sammy clasped her fiancé's hands in a gesture of supplication and said, 'I don't want you to end up in prison, Kelvin.'

'I won't. I'm not stupid. I'm a very good burglar.'

'You say your father was a good one, but he still got caught.'

'Well, I'm a better burglar than he was.'

'Oh, so now you're going into competition with the dead, are you?'

'No, I'm not,' he said angrily. 'I'm respecting his memory.'

'And you feel the best way you can do that is by "going into the family business"?'

'Yes, I do. And in most cases where sons follow their fathers into family businesses they have the opportunity to learn the tricks of the trade at their old man's knee. Well, thanks to my bloody mother's intervention and my father's early death I was prevented from having those opportunities. I've had to learn everything for myself.'

'Yes, but what worries me, Kelvin, is that what you do for a living is going to ruin our relationship.' Sammy sounded desperate now.

'No, it won't. I've told you. I won't go to prison because I won't get caught.'

'But what's going to happen . . . I mean, if we have children? Are we going to tell them what their dad does for a living?'

'Of course we are, Sammy. I'm not going to repeat the mistakes my parents made into another generation. Our kids are going to grow up proud of what their dad does.'

'So do you mean you're planning to go on being a burglar forever?'

'Yes,' said Kelvin Stockett with gratified contentment. 'I've got so much time to make up. Remember, I only found out about what my father had done in life when I was clearing up the stuff after my mother's death. So I owe him a lot for those many years when I had no idea what he did.'

'You mean I can't look forward *ever* to a time when you're not a burglar?'

'No, Sammy. As I've told you before,' he replied with great firmness. 'And can we please say that that's the last word on the subject? I want to enjoy our evening together.'

'Yes, but . . . oh . . .' She couldn't help saying the words. 'It just seems such a waste.'

'Are you saying that my old man wasted his life?'

'No, I'm not. But it's different for you. You didn't have to become a burglar, while your father probably did. You had all the advantages. You went to public school, you got a very good degree in Mechanical Engineering at Cambridge. There are any number of jobs you are qualified for.'

'But none of them are jobs that pay tribute to the achievements of my father.'

'I know, but . . .' Sammy Pinkerton pushed her chair back. She was on the verge of tears, and she knew Kelvin never liked to see her crying. 'I'm going home.'

'But you haven't finished your wine.'

'No, but . . . I'm going.'

'I'll just finish my pint and be with you,' Kelvin called to her retreating back.

He wasn't really worried about her departure. He knew they'd make it up again back at the flat. In bed. They were very good at making things up in bed. They were meant for each other.

They both knew that. And both drew a strong feeling of security from that knowledge.

It was really only that one thing they argued about. Kelvin's occupation . . . or, in his view, his vocation. Their verbal tussles on the subject were tiresome, but he felt confident that Sammy would eventually come round to his way of thinking.

He certainly had no plans to change. Every successful burglary he committed was not only a celebration of his father's life, it was also one in the eye for the mother for whom, since her death, his hatred had only increased.

When he emerged from the pub Kelvin Stockett did not notice the broad-shouldered man who levered himself off the wall and sauntered after him. Nor was he aware that he was being followed until at the end of his road the man grew closer and spoke his name.

'Yes, that's me,' Kelvin admitted cautiously. Though none of his burglaries had ever involved violence, he knew that the world in which he now operated was a criminal one where a high degree of caution was advisable.

'Kelvin Stockett the burglar?' asked the man.

After his recent assertions of pride in his occupation he was not about to deny that. The man didn't have the air of a member of the police force. Too well-spoken, for a start.

'I think I might have a job for you, Kelvin.'

'A burglary job?'

'Oh yes.'

'What is it? And, come to that, who are you?'

'My name,' said the man, 'is Edmund Grainger.'

Mrs Pargeter was not a great enthusiast of the television. She knew that a great many widows found it a great comfort in their loneliness, but that was very much the kind of widow she had no intention of being.

She and her late husband had watched very little when he was alive – except, of course, for police press conferences. Neither she nor the late Mr Pargeter had ever followed fictional crime series. They both found them all rather tame. And deeply implausible.

But, although she'd never considered having a television in her bedroom (it was far too pretty a room), she did have one downstairs in the sitting room which she would occasionally switch on to see the BBC news.

And so it was that on Thursday evening she heard another reference to Sir Normington Winthrop. It was quarter to eleven, and she had missed the nightly chronicling of the day's disasters, so she switched on *Newsnight* . . . where she found one of its feistier female presenters called Jenny Nagle interviewing a plump man who was vaguely familiar from the newspapers but to whom she couldn't put a name.

Obligingly, the presenter identified him as Derek Bardon, leader of BROG, the 'Britons, Restore Our Greatness' party. (Why was it, Mrs Pargeter wondered, that all minority political groupings had such silly names? UKIP, she'd always thought, sounded like an invitation to go to sleep – and having listened to the party's candidates outlining their policies she'd frequently felt encouraged to do just that.)

Anyway, remembering the connection between the late Sir Normington Winthrop and BROG, Mrs Pargeter listened with increased concentration to what its leader was saying.

'It sounds to me as if your researchers have let you down, Jenny.' Though this was undoubtedly a criticism, Derek Bardon's tone was not harsh. He was using the voice a dog-lover would use to an overexcited puppy. 'Those accusations of racism within BROG were put to bed a good three years ago. There was a full internal inquiry, which resulted in the expulsion of two – only two, Jenny – members of the party. I absolutely defy you now to find any evidence of racism amongst our membership – or, indeed, in our policies.'

Jenny Nagle, an attractive woman with expertly highlighted long brown hair, was not about to be patronised in that way. She came back at him strongly. 'But surely even the name of the party – "Britons, Restore Our Greatness" – has overtones of at least jingoism, harking back to the glory days of the British Empire?'

'You may feel that, Jenny, but I can assure you that there is no nostalgia in BROG for what you call "the glory days of the British Empire". We have no plans to recolonize the world. Our only aim is to bring back Great Britain's self-respect – a self-respect which has been eroded in the last thirty years by the attitudes of a series of governments led by this country's two main parties. That, Jenny, is all that BROG is trying to achieve.'

He was good, Mrs Pargeter could see that. Good in the way that all media-savvy politicians had to be. His constant use of the presenter's name; his avuncular manner which stayed just the right side of patronizing, while still managing to emphasize her relative youth and inexperience.

'Jenny,' he said, continuing the same approach, 'I'm not really a politician. I don't share the ambitions that most politicians have. I'm just an ordinary Joe, the man in the street, the man, if you like, on the Clapham Omnibus – and that dates me, doesn't it? But all I'm trying to do, all that BROG is trying to do, Jenny, is to bring a little *common sense* into British political life. As I say, I don't share the ambitions of most politicians, but I look around and I see so many things wrong with this great country of ours. What I don't see, though, Jenny, is anyone rolling up their shirtsleeves to put those things right. Everyone seems quite happy to sit back and watch Great Britain degenerate into a third world country. Well, I'm not like that. I see a mess, I immediately want to sort it out. That's why I'm involved in the mucky business of politics. That's why I'm the leader of BROG.'

It was one of the oldest populist stances in the book – the man of the people who simply wants to do good and realizes, to his great frustration, that he can only be in a position to make changes by entering the murky waters of politics. But Mrs Pargeter had to admit Derek Bardon played the role quite well.

The presenter, Jenny Nagle, also had that feeling and was anxious to move her interview on. 'Could we, Derek, talk about the late Sir Normington Winthrop?'

'Of course we could, Jenny. A very fine man who will be sorely missed.'

'I'm sure. But he'll be particularly sorely missed by BROG, won't he?'

'Of course.'

'Because, in a sense, didn't he give respectability to the party?'

'I'm sorry, Jenny. I'm not with you.'

'Well, in the early days BROG was dismissed by some people as a collection of crackpots and misfits.'

'Not by any people I ever met, Jenny.'

'Well, that suggests to me that you don't see many people, Derek. That maybe you ought to get out more.'

He was offended by that. But before he could shape a response, the presenter pressed on: 'So it was useful for your party to have an establishment figure like Sir Normington Winthrop on board. He enhanced your image, didn't he?'

'All I know, Jenny,' said Derek Bardon, his coolness regained, 'is that I was proud to have Norm in my party. He was one of our core supporters. He was part of the BROG vision from the very moment I had the idea for the party.'

'Without Sir Normington Winthrop there wouldn't be a BROG?'

'No, there wouldn't, Jenny. Not in its current form.'

He had fallen into her little trap. 'Because, in fact,' she said triumphantly, 'Sir Normington Winthrop funded the entire operation, didn't he?'

Derek Bardon didn't like that either. Across his face there flashed a considerably less avuncular look: a look almost of pure evil. It was only there for a second before the politician's instinct reasserted itself.

'We do have other donors, Jenny,' he said smoothly. 'While hugely grateful for what Norm did for us – and what he did for the party in so many ways – I can assure you, Jenny, that his absence – though very sad for me personally – will in no way affect the future success of BROG. We have got a lot of forward momentum in the party and, come the next election, Jenny, BROG is going to be a force to be reckoned with throughout the country.'

The presenter looked as if she wanted to ask more, but time was against her. She thanked Derek Bardon and moved on to introduce the next item, about the government's plans to reduce subsidies on the installation of stairlifts for the elderly.

The last shot of Derek Bardon showed him looking triumphant.

*   *   *

Up in her bedroom, reaching round to unzip her dress, Mrs Pargeter suddenly remembered what she still had in her handbag. Gizmo Gilbert's latest invention. The 'Zipper Zapper'.

She held it over her shoulder and pressed the button. Her dress instantly unzipped itself.

It was a really useful device. With the proper marketing . . . As she drifted into the sleep of the righteous, Mrs Pargeter wondered whether there'd be the name of someone in her little black book who was an expert in starting up companies. There almost definitely would be.

THIRTEEN

She rang Truffler Mason first thing the next morning. 'I'm in a state of confusion,' she said.

'That's unlike you, Mrs P. I always think of you as being positive under any circumstances.'

'Yes, I try to be. But my current circumstances aren't making me feel very positive.'

'What's wrong?' There was genuine alarm in the private investigator's voice.

'No, it's nothing to worry about on a cosmic scale. I just feel frustrated because I've got all these leads wiggling off in different directions and I can't get any of them to join together. There's Sir Normington Winthrop's link to my husband; there's Holy Smirke being kidnapped . . . Oh, I'd just like to be able to join them all together, make a few connections, see a way forward.'

'Doing an investigation's often like that,' said Truffler with what was meant to sound like reassurance. 'Just at the very moment when you think you're never going to make sense of it, you get a breakthrough. Remember, they always say that the darkest hour is just before dawn.'

'Do you really believe that, Truffler?'

His natural pessimism reasserted itself. 'No. Mind you, I can inform you of some progress. I wouldn't go as far as to call it a breakthrough, but it might be worth pursuing.'

'What is it?' asked Mrs Pargeter eagerly.

'Well, you know I've been employed by Lady Winthrop to try and find out as much as I can about her husband's origins.'

'Yes. Which is more or less exactly what I'm trying to do.' Again, she sounded excited. 'Why, have you got something?'

'Not really. He seems to have kept his wife in complete ignorance about his background, certainly his early days. But what you just said . . . I'd been thinking about that too.'

'Which bit of what I just said?'

'The bit about you and Lady Winthrop both investigating the same thing.'

'Oh?'

'I suggested to her that it might be a good idea if the two of you met – you know, that you should pool your resources.'

'Not that I've currently got many resources to pool.' But she was only downcast for a moment. 'I still think it's a brilliant idea, though, Truffler.'

She recalled the chilling threat in Edmund Grainger's phone call when he'd told her not to contact Lady Winthrop, but she wasn't the kind of woman to be daunted by considerations like that. She knew she was being perverse, but she was determined that she wasn't going to let a bully win. 'Can you arrange for us to meet this afternoon?' she asked Truffler.

''Course I can, Mrs P.'

She had a call soon after that from Erin Jarvis. The girl said she'd thought of a new line of enquiry. 'You remember, Mrs Pargeter, you told me that Holy Smirke had known your husband since schooldays?'

'Yes.'

'Well, I thought of doing a bit of research into where they went to school. Obviously, if Holy Smirke was around we could ask him, but for equally obvious reasons we can't.'

'I think that's a really good idea, Erin. And in your researches you might also find out whether there were any other, er, associates of my husband who he knew all that way back.' Suddenly, she saw a snag. 'Trouble is, though, my husband never talked to me about those days. I don't even know the name of the school he went to.'

'Don't worry, Mrs Pargeter,' said Erin coolly. 'I've already found that out.'

Greene's Hotel turned out to be a convenient location for Lady Winthrop, and she was at least as keen as Mrs Pargeter for their meeting to take place. So they arranged to meet for coffee in the Blenheim Room at three thirty.

Arriving before the appointed hour, Mrs Pargeter was greeted by Hedgeclipper Clinton, who asked if she wanted her

customary bottle of champagne. She could think of no reason
to oppose the suggestion, so was halfway down the first glass
when her guest arrived.

Having only seen Helena Winthrop on the occasion of her
husband's funeral, when she had been decorously swathed in
black, Mrs Pargeter found her to be younger and prettier than
she'd remembered. The blondness of the woman's hair had only
been slightly assisted. She wore very high heels and a well-cut
suit in a shade of scarlet that a lot of women couldn't have got
away with.

When she spoke, her vowels were as cut-glass as the glasses
from which they were drinking their champagne. (Lady Winthrop
had made no demur about the substitution of the promised
coffee.)

Mrs Pargeter started with a formal condolence for the loss
of Sir Normington Winthrop.

'Thank you. I'm sorry that we didn't get introduced at the
funeral. I gather from Mr Mason that you, too, are widowed.'

'Yes. My husband died quite a long time ago, though.'

'And is time the great healer that people promise it to be?'

'It does help a bit . . . though, of course, one never fully
recovers. But I feel that it's very important not to just live on
one's memories.'

'No. Not that I'm really sure about the memories I might
have to live on.'

Mrs Pargeter looked puzzled. 'I don't quite know what you
mean, Lady Winthrop.'

'Oh, please call me Helena.'

'Very well, Helena. But what did you mean about your
memories?'

'Well, the more I find out about my husband's past, the less
I feel that I really knew him at all. There are whole areas of
his life of which I was completely ignorant.'

'Ah.' Some people might have thought that the same was
true of Mrs Pargeter's marriage, but she was entirely confident
that that had not been the case. Yes, there were details of the
late Mr Pargeter's business affairs of which she knew nothing,
but that had been for shrewd, pragmatic reasons. 'What you
do not know about, Melita my love,' he had frequently said to

her, 'cannot be extracted from you, even by torture.' Fortunately, torture had never been involved, but there had been occasions when, questioned about her late husband's activities, she'd had cause to be grateful for her ignorance.

Mrs Pargeter went on: 'I, too, am very interested in your husband's past, as I'm sure Truffler has told you.'

'I'm sorry? Who's Truffler?'

'Ah. I mean Mr Mason of the Mason De Vere Detective Agency. He is universally known as Truffler.'

'Oh.' A small smile crossed Helena Winthrop's face. 'What a very suitable nickname. I won't be able to think of him as anything else now. Will he mind if I call him Truffler?'

'He'll be delighted if you do.'

'Good.' There was a silence. Helena Winthrop seemed somewhat nervous of what she was about to say. 'May I ask you, Mrs Pargeter, *why* you are interested in my late husband's past?'

There was no reason not to tell the truth, so Mrs Pargeter explained about the name 'Normington Winthrop' appearing in the invaluable little black book which her husband had bequeathed to her. 'And it's such an unusual name. I cannot imagine there being many Normington Winthrops in the world.'

'No,' Helena agreed. 'That is an odd coincidence. It suggests that our husbands must at one stage have known each other.'

'That would seem to be the logical conclusion, yes. So how far back can you trace your husband's history?'

'Well, only since he arrived in this country from Africa.'

'Africa?' Mrs Pargeter echoed with considerable surprise.

'Yes. Normington had worked in the Congo. I think it was there that he made his first fortune. And, I believe, married his first wife.'

'Really? Did you ever meet her?'

'No. She didn't come to England with him. Maybe she died in Africa. Maybe they were divorced. I've no idea.'

'But your husband was brought up in England, wasn't he?'

'That I'm not absolutely sure about, but I rather think not. Though he never positively confirmed it, he gave me the impression that he was brought up in South Africa.'

'Did he speak with a South African accent?'

'No. He spoke quite respectably after a while. Another of the reasons he married me, I think, to improve his vowels.'

'But when he first came to England, did he have a South African accent then?'

'No. Then his accent was just –' with a slight shudder – 'uncouth. I'm surprised you never heard him speak.'

'Well, I didn't.'

'Not even on television? Extolling the virtues of the BROG party?'

'I didn't, no, but by coincidence I did hear Derek Bardon talking on *Newsnight* last night.' Helena Winthrop's shudder was more evocative than any words would have been.

'Not your favourite person?'

'No. I really have no idea why Normington involved himself in that nonsense.'

'Didn't he ever tell you?'

'No. That was another subject on which his lips were sealed.'

'And how long ago was it that he settled in this country?'

'Seventeen years. We met soon after he arrived.'

'And where did you meet? I always like to hear people's romantic stories.'

Helena Winthrop's face took on a hard look. 'Ours was not, I'm afraid, that romantic. When he arrived in this country, Normington had a great deal of money but very little class. That's what he was hoping to acquire by marrying me.'

'Oh?'

'I do have a title in my own right. I'm not just a lady because of his knighthood. But my family were classic aristocrats. Lots of class, family tree going back to the Norman Conquest, but never two pennies to rub together. Normington offered a way out of that. And I was pushing forty, not overwhelmed with other offers . . . so I thought our pragmatically sensible relationship might turn into love. It didn't.'

'I'm sorry.'

'Oh, there were compensations . . . not having to worry about money all the time being the main one. And I fulfilled my side of the bargain. Acted as the perfect consort and hostess, eased Normington way up the ladder of respectability. I'm sure there have been many worse marriages.'

'Maybe,' said Mrs Pargeter.

'This may, incidentally, explain why you don't find me prostrated with grief. The main feeling Normington's death prompted in me was relief.'

Always interested in the possibility of foul play, Mrs Pargeter said, 'Do you mind if I ask how your husband died?'

'Prostate cancer. He'd had it for some years. Had lots of treatments which staved off the inevitable for a while, but it finally caught up with him.'

'So not unexpected?'

'Absolutely not.'

Mrs Pargeter nodded thoughtfully, then gestured to a hovering waiter to fill up their glasses. 'We're still no nearer finding out how our husbands met, are we?'

'No.'

'What really intrigues me, though, is what your late husband got up to in Africa.'

'It intrigues me too,' said Lady Winthrop.

FOURTEEN

She was back in the Chigwell house that Friday evening, looking with distaste at the pink and white china cat on the mantelpiece and wondering how she could get rid of it without hurting Gary's feelings, when she had a call from Erin Jarvis. 'I've found out quite a lot about your husband's schooldays.'

'Wow! That was quick.'

'I am quick.' The claim wasn't boastful. It was just a statement of fact. 'He went to Cheesemongers' First School till he was eleven and then moved on to Cheesemongers' Hall.'

'That sounds very grand.'

'It wasn't at all. Both schools were in the East End – been knocked down years ago and replaced with tower blocks. And they provided state education in its most basic form. None of the pupils went on to any kind of college or university. All left at sixteen . . . and many much earlier. The truancy rates were very high, and a lot of them were working full-time in family businesses by the time they were fourteen. Anyway, I managed to track down the attendance registers and other records for both schools.'

Mrs Pargeter had a strong temptation to ask how on earth Erin had managed to do that so quickly, but she restrained herself. The girl's professional secrets must be respected.

'Well,' Erin went on, 'what the registers reveal is that your husband and another boy called Richard Smirke—'

'That must be Holy.'

'I reckon so. Anyway, they were together through both schools. Actually started on the same day.'

'Oh, it's very frustrating not being able to talk to Holy, isn't it? I do hope nothing terrible's happened to him.'

'If Napper Johnson's on the case, he'll find him,' said Erin firmly, ruling out less attractive possibilities.

'I hope so. Sorry, Erin. You were saying that the two of them went through both schools together . . .?'

'Yes, and their reports suggest that neither of them . . .' The girl chose her words carefully. 'That neither of them were particularly interested in their studies.'

'Ah.'

'But they were always together, and it was like they had their own little gang.'

'Really?'

'In fact,' Erin went on boldly, 'one of their teachers said that in her view both of the young men were destined for a life of crime.'

'What a strange thing to say,' Mrs Pargeter observed innocently.

'Yes. But the interesting detail is that there was a third member of their gang as well.'

'And his name wouldn't, by any chance, have been Normington Winthrop?' asked Mrs Pargeter eagerly.

'Wouldn't that have been neat? But no, the third member of the gang was called Tony Hardcastle.'

'Never heard the name. Just a minute.' Mrs Pargeter reached into her handbag. 'Wait while I check whether there's a Tony Hardcastle in my husband's little black book.' She flicked through the pages. 'Oh yes, there is something here. Tony Hardcastle. Under "Armourers".'

'And is it one of the first names in the category?'

'No. That's "Normington Winthrop", as we know. Tony Hardcastle comes quite a long way down the list. The ink's a lot less faded than on the names above him. Also there's a line through him. He's been crossed out.'

'And you say that usually means the person has died?'

'I think so, Erin, yes.'

'Hm. Well, it would make sense for the name to be under "Armourers".'

'Oh?'

'There was a big fuss at Cheesemongers' Hall when twelve-year-old Tony Hardcastle was discovered to have brought a gun into school one day.'

'Blimey.'

'An old service revolver someone had nicked during the war. It apparently caused a major panic.'

'And this Tony Hardcastle was part of the gang with my husband and Holy Smirke?'

'Very definitely. He was included in the list of those who that one teacher reckoned were destined for a life of crime.'

'Right. I wonder what happened to him . . .?'

'I'll try to find out, but there seems to be no record of him anywhere. Actually, I had a thought, Mrs Pargeter . . .'

'What was that, love?'

'You remember when we were looking through all the original records that my dad had kept?'

'Yes.'

'And we found that some bits had been cut out?'

'I remember.'

'Well, we assumed those were references to Normington Winthrop.'

'Yes.'

'But perhaps it's more likely, given what we know now, that they were actually references to Tony Hardcastle.'

'It's possible, yes.'

'Because in all the records I checked from Cheesemongers' First School and Cheesemongers' Hall there was no reference anywhere to Normington Winthrop.'

Which, thought Mrs Pargeter, was hardly surprising if he was brought up in South Africa.

She felt more confused than ever.

FIFTEEN

'It could be arson,' Edmund Grainger suggested.

'No, I don't do arson,' said Kelvin Stockett firmly. 'I'm a burglar.'

'Maybe just as well. If you actually bring the stuff to us then we'll be sure no one else can lay their hands on it.'

'And you reckon it'll all be on the one laptop?'

'Yes, but they'll probably have made back-ups – external hard drives, memory sticks. I want you to clear out all that stuff.'

'No problem.'

They were sitting in an anonymous pub near Clapham Junction on Saturday afternoon. Country and western music whinged too loudly from the speakers, but at least ensured that no one could overhear their conversation.

'And if you do this assignment all right, Kelvin, there could be more work coming your way.'

'From your organization?'

'Yes.'

'Sort of like having a permanent job?' asked Kelvin, remembering his recent conversation with Sammy.

'I'm not sure about that. Why do you ask?'

'Oh, nothing, don't worry about it. Incidentally, what does your organization actually *do*, Mr Grainger?'

'I don't think there's any need for you to know that.'

'Very well.' Kelvin Stockett didn't argue.

'And I want the job done quickly. In fact, remember the fee we agreed?'

Kelvin nodded. There was no danger of his forgetting that in a hurry. It was a very substantial sum.

'Well,' Edmund Grainger went on, 'each day the job hasn't got done a grand gets knocked off that fee.'

'So there's a real incentive for me to get it done sharpish.'

'I'd say so.'

'Right.' That, in fact, suited Kelvin Stockett well. Sammy

Pinkerton would not be in their flat that night. It was her hen party, and Mrs Pargeter had booked all the participants into Greene's Hotel, so that when in the small hours they stumbled out of the final club they wouldn't have to bother about getting taxis home.

Kelvin grinned as he said, 'Tell me where the properties I've got to break into are.'

The man gave him the two addresses.

Edmund Grainger waited about twenty minutes after Kelvin had left the pub, then he left for the dull suburban house in the hinterland of Lavender Hill where Holy Smirke was being kept captive. The vicar had already been very helpful in providing details of Mrs Pargeter's connections – like the addresses he had just given to Kelvin Stockett – but Edmund Grainger felt certain there was more information to come. He didn't think it'd be too difficult to extract it from the old man. A little persuasion was all that would be required, and Edmund Grainger was a master of the arts of persuasion.

Mrs Pargeter was surprised how sedate Sammy Pinkerton's hen night guests were when they arrived. Most of them had checked into Greene's about five on the Saturday afternoon and spent a couple of hours exploring each other's rooms, dressing and titivating for the evening ahead. Hairstyles were experimented with, faces were painted in a variety of styles, eyelashes and a profusion of glitter were stuck on.

All of this activity was conducted to a soundtrack of much giggling, but nobody got raucous. Perhaps they were holding something back for later in the evening.

Mrs Pargeter had offered to organize dinner at Greene's for all of them. Her plan had been to stay at home in Chigwell for the evening, but Sammy Pinkerton wouldn't hear of it. 'You've done so much, you've been so much a part of my wedding plans, that I really do want you there at my hen night.'

After a little more argument Mrs Pargeter had been convinced that Sammy meant what she said and agreed to attend the dinner. 'But going on to the clubs afterwards . . . I don't think that's for me.'

'You'll love it, Mrs Pargeter.'

'My presence will double the average age in places like that.'

'Don't you worry about a thing. Age is just a number.'

Mrs Pargeter didn't worry when young people used that line, but she found it embarrassing to hear from her contemporaries. It usually came from women of the mutton-dressed-as-lamb tendency and contained elements of protesting too much. Mrs Pargeter knew exactly how old she was, and that was the age she felt. But she never let her advancing years inhibit her acute enjoyment of life.

'Well, I'll join you for the dinner and at the end of the meal make a decision about the rest of the evening.'

'I've already made that decision for you, Mrs Pargeter.'

The dinner was served in Greene's Hotel's private Ramillies Suite. Seated next to Sammy, Mrs Pargeter looked along the table with great affection and a degree of pride. Apart from Erin she hadn't met any of the guests before, but they had all introduced themselves with great politeness. In their glad rags they looked absolutely stunning, but the bride-to-be's dark beauty outshone them all (which was exactly as it should be).

Mrs Pargeter raised her glass of champagne. 'To the beginning,' she said, 'of what I'm sure will be a brilliant evening!'

Kelvin Stockett eased the Ford Transit van along the wet streets of South London. He had chosen carefully where he stole the vehicle from, eventually deciding on a transport parking compound owned by one of the high street banks. He knew that while they were very zealous about security in their actual branch buildings, they were relatively slack about protecting their peripheral services, so he reckoned breaking into the place would not be too much of a problem. As for alarms on the actual vehicle . . . well, he had ways of dealing with those.

This first part of the theft went like clockwork. Getting himself inside the compound offered no problems at all. Nor was it difficult to break into the Portakabin office to extract the relevant key.

He had taken with him magnetic number plates to put over

his real ones, and he used the old trick of putting different registrations on the front and the back of the van. This could arouse unwelcome curiosity if the vehicle was parked for any length of time during the day, but when driving about by night it was a useful way of confusing witnesses.

The other big advantage of his choice of venue for the theft was that very few bank staff worked at weekends.

Driving the Transit out of the compound was easy, and when that was done he carefully closed and re-padlocked the gates so there'd be no signs of his illegal entrance and exit.

He had cased the two joints during the day and reckoned the back way was going to be favourite in both. The problems he envisaged were not to do with breaking in – he had honed his skills to such a level that there was hardly a building in London that he couldn't have got into – but were more concerned with the amount of material he'd have to take away from both crime scenes. And until he got inside he wouldn't actually know how much stuff there was.

Behind the first building was a small yard backed by a brick wall with a wooden gate in it. There was a space right outside, perfect for parking the Transit.

He sat for a moment, gathering his concentration for the task that lay ahead. The rain was now falling more heavily, which brought with it both a disadvantage and an advantage. Wet drainpipes and window sills would make climbing more hazardous. But on the bonus side, the weather would keep most potential witnesses indoors.

Though the rain was so hard, he didn't put on anything waterproof. That would only make his body more slick and slippery. A black hoodie was less dangerous (and also hid his distinctively blond hair). Black jeans, black trainers with ridged soles that could grip on any surface. Black scarf across the lower part of his face. Black gloves with rubber ribbing across the palms and fingers.

The feeble padlock on the wooden gate offered little resistance. Inside the small yard he managed to heave himself up to a second-floor window sill on which he edged along towards the drainpipe.

This didn't look as robust as he would have wished. When

he touched the metal, the pipe rattled slightly in its fixings. But Kelvin knew he'd have to risk it. There was no other way he was going to make it up to the third floor.

He was very fit and a good climber, and he soon found himself adjacent to the window through which he wanted to enter the building. For reasons of noise and professional pride he had no desire to break the window, but fortunately he managed to jemmy it up without leaving a mark.

He slipped into the office and whipped out his torch. The beam travelled round the room, causing him to let out an involuntary whistle at the amount of stuff there was and in what chaos it was scattered. Though his fee was large, he was certainly going to earn it.

His torch beam landed on a wall chart calendar, its dates empty of stickers or notes of bookings. But the words picked out above it in stick-on gold letters confirmed that he had come to the right place.

They read 'MASON DE VERE DETECTIVE AGENCY'.

Of course, when it came to it and they had finished their excellent dinner at Greene's Hotel, there was no question of Mrs Pargeter returning straight away to Chigwell.

The bouncer on the door of the first club they visited looked slightly askance at her when she made to enter. ''Ere,' he said, 'you're not meant to bring your mums along.'

'Mrs Pargeter is my guest,' said Sammy Pinkerton forcefully.

'Also,' the subject of the argument pointed out, 'I am no one's mum. I am a person in my own right, which is why I'm going to walk straight past you and enter this club.'

The bouncer was so flabbergasted that he just unhooked the velvet rope and let her in.

Inside, the music was so loud that speech was impossible. But Mrs Pargeter was soon moving sinuously to the beat.

So sinuously that it wasn't long before a rather good-looking young man started to dance with her.

Funny, thought Mrs Pargeter, I've never thought of myself as a cougar . . . but for one night, who cares?

* * *

One of the early lessons Kelvin Stockett had learned as a burglar was that one should not always try to attain invisibility. Being seen while you're working is not invariably a bad thing. If members of the public see someone confidently walking around, apparently doing his job, they tend not to find his or her actions suspicious.

He put this experience to good use in removing all of Truffler Mason's files. He switched the lights on in the office and on the stairs down to the back yard. He left the back door and the wooden gate open as he kept going in for another load. He left the Transit's sidelights on and its back gates open. He even whistled while he worked.

Though he felt quite confident about what he was doing, he was still glad that there weren't many potential witnesses around. A couple of old men taking their dogs out to do their business took no notice of him. And a courting couple with arms all over each other showed no interest either.

Because of the volume of stuff, transferring it all from office to van took over an hour. Packing it all in the back of the Transit took time too. He piled it up carefully to leave as much space as possible. He didn't know how much he'd be removing from his next port of call.

Mrs Pargeter thought they were in the third club – or it might have been the fourth. The sedate young ladies of the dinner at Greene's Hotel were now rather less sedate but, though they had shed any vestige of inhibition, none of them had yet become too raucous, maudlin or drunk. They were just having a good time.

And Mrs Pargeter was having as good a time as any of them, matching dance move for dance move, downing shot for shot, and still a magnet for young men.

At one of the clubs – or possibly someone had brought them from Greene's Hotel – they had acquired bunny ears and devil's horns. Mrs Pargeter, wearing the latter, was bopping away when Erin approached her through the gyrating crowd. Her bunny ears were a little askew, and her purple hair had come to little sweaty points on her forehead.

'It's after four, Mrs P,' she shouted above the din. 'I think I'd better be going.'

'Oh, don't do that now,' Mrs Pargeter bellowed back. 'There's a room waiting for you back at Greene's.'

'But I was intending to get home.'

'How long's that going to take you?'

'Half an hour, if I can find a cab.'

'From here we can walk to Greene's in five minutes,' Mrs Pargeter roared back. 'Stay.'

'Oh, all right,' said Erin, drifting back through the throng into the arms of a young man who appeared to be literally panting for her.

Mrs Pargeter straightened her devil's horns and continued dancing.

The Transit van drew up round the back of the house that used to belong to Jukebox Jarvis. Kelvin Stockett knew that a different kind of caution was required here. The Mason De Vere Detective Agency had been in an area of shops and offices with not many people around on a Saturday night. And although Sammy had told him that Erin herself would be away at the hen party, he still had to be vigilant. Now he was in suburbia, home of nosy neighbours and twitching curtains. Also, he suspected, from what he'd managed to find out about Erin Jarvis, that her security systems might be more sophisticated than Truffler's.

He stayed in the Transit a good ten minutes before making any move and was relieved to see that no lights were switched on in the adjacent houses. Then he slipped out of the van, silently closing its door.

The wall at the back of the garden fortunately had a gate in it, padlocked on the inside. Shinning over the wall proved easy for someone as fit as Kelvin. Once inside he used an old-fashioned picklock to deal with the padlock.

There was sufficient moonlight for him to see that he was in a very well-kept garden. He advanced across it towards the kitchen door.

When he was very close he took out his tiny torch and inspected the locks. He recognized the brand immediately from the extensive research he had done into commercially available security systems. Disabling the lock and getting into the house would not be a problem, but then he knew he'd only have thirty seconds to find and switch off the alarm.

He brought his torch beam close to the kitchen window and checked out the interior geography. He couldn't see the alarm control box on the walls and reasoned, from his considerable experience of such things, that it was more likely to be at the front of the house. There was only one door leading off the kitchen, which he reckoned must lead to the hall. So he'd have to get through that door, find the alarm control and switch it off – all within his allotted thirty seconds.

If he was wrong about where he anticipated finding the box, then his evening's mission would have to be aborted.

But Kelvin Stockett didn't allow in any negative thoughts when he was working. And when he was doing a burglary job he felt more alive than he did at any other time. He was supremely confident in his own abilities. That's how he knew it was the right career for him. Just as it had been for his father.

He took a couple of deep breaths. Then he removed a small electronic zapper from his pocket. Pointing it at the lock, he pressed the button.

With a very quiet bleep the kitchen door opened. His ribbed soles silent on the tiled floor, he dashed across the room, opened the door and found himself, as he had hoped, in a narrow hallway. And there on the wall, just at the bottom of the stairs, was fixed a metal box from which an admonitory red LED light blinked at him.

It was a matter of seconds to open the metal cover and switch the alarm off. Fortunately, he knew a way of doing this which bypassed the keypad code. He looked at his watch. Easy. He'd done it with four seconds to spare.

Now securely inside the house, he took his time to look around. The front room appeared to be an office, where the only evidence of any archive system was a gleaming state-of-the-art laptop.

Kelvin checked the thickness and extent of the blind on the main window and decided he could risk putting the lights on. Then he sat down in front of the laptop and, using a long numerical code to bypass the password, logged on. He checked out what backup systems were being used and keyed in another long numerical code which would erase all data that had been saved on Erin's iCloud.

He then went around the room meticulously collecting memory sticks and any other electronic components which might possibly be used for storage purposes. He felt a self-congratulatory glow. This was going to be a lot easier than the raid on Truffler Mason's office had been.

But when he looked in the back room, that confidence very quickly faded. The space was absolutely filled with library shelves of files – old cardboard files in only marginally better condition than the ones from Truffler's place that were already filling half the Transit.

But there was no way he could give up now. Edmund Grainger's directions had been very specific, and if Kelvin was going to claim the large fee that had been agreed he would have to clear all archival material that he found in Erin Jarvis's house.

He settled down to the task, trying to get his mind into an attitude of Zen acceptance. Each file he moved out into the garden was one he wouldn't have to move again (or, at least, only from the garden to the Transit).

Transferring the stuff was back-breaking toil which took him over three hours. But finally it was all crammed in and with relief he could lock the Transit's back doors.

He then went back into the house to check that he hadn't missed anything. Using another special code, he reset the burglar alarm and relocked both the back door and the garden gate.

Dawn strips of lighter grey were appearing in the sky as he drove towards the address he'd been given off Lavender Hill. And though he was totally exhausted, Kelvin Stockett felt the satisfaction of a job well done.

SIXTEEN

When he was busy on an investigation, Truffler Mason didn't take much notice of weekends. He didn't take much notice of them even when he wasn't busy on an investigation. His flat was a dingy, unadorned place with none of those little personal touches that make a home. So the more time he spent away from it, the better.

It was no surprise then that nine o'clock on the Sunday morning found him putting the key in the lock of the book-maker's beneath which his office was located.

Once inside, it didn't take him long to realize that he'd had a visitor. It was so long since he had been able to see the floor through all the clutter that he had forgotten the hideous pink linoleum that covered it.

He lowered his long body into his ancient swivel chair and surveyed the emptiness around him. Though furious, he couldn't suppress a small feeling of sneaky admiration for the thorough job his visitor had done.

He tried to shut his mind to the effects the theft would have on his working life, the amount of irreplaceable data he had lost, and concentrate instead on trying to work out who might have committed the crime.

Truffler Mason's line of work was one in which making enemies went with the territory. So he tried to think which of them he had recently offended. But, of course, the crime was not just a random act of vandalism. The perpetrator had not taken his phone, laptop or any other office equipment. All he had wanted was the private investigator's files: the archive of his professional life.

That suggested it was not the action of someone for whom Truffler's investigations had led to the closing-down of a lucra-tive criminal enterprise, or even to an arrest. For them, the archive would already have done its worst.

No, it had to be the work of someone who was *currently*

under investigation. And the case Truffler was working on at that time, on behalf of Mrs Pargeter and Lady Winthrop, was the discovery of the secrets of Sir Normington Winthrop's past. That had to be the connection to the theft of all his files.

But though he reckoned his logic was impeccable, it didn't bring him any nearer to putting a name to the burglar in question.

Truffler looked around his bare office, his face more mournful than ever, and tried to think of some work he could do that didn't involve consulting his files. Only one thought occurred to him. He picked up the phone and dialled Napper Johnson's mobile number.

He knew the PR consultant didn't work weekends, and indeed had a rather classy social life, spent on people's yachts or in house parties at stately homes. But he reckoned he should still be able to make contact on the mobile.

His supposition proved correct. Napper answered on the third ring, his voice as ever marinated in suavity.

Truffler Mason identified himself and said, 'Sorry to trouble you at the weekend, but I was thinking it's been a while since we've heard from you.'

'You don't have to tell me that. I am all too well aware of my shortcomings on the case. I thought if we just followed the trail of the CCTV cameras we'd find out immediately where your kidnapped vicar was being held and have rescued him by the end of the day. Sadly, I discovered we were up against rather more sophisticated villains than I had first thought.'

'How'd you mean?'

'They, too, appear able to hack into the Metropolitan and City police CCTV systems.'

'Oh?'

'This is rather embarrassing for me to say, Truffler. They've made me look like an idiot.'

'I didn't think it was possible to do that, Napper.'

'Thank you very much for your confidence. Sadly, in this case it is misplaced.'

'So what did they do?'

'My staff were tracking the kidnappers' car perfectly easily . . . until it got south of the river.'

'What happened then?'

'As soon as the vehicle crossed Battersea Bridge, the CCTV feed stopped and was replaced by a video.'

'A video of what?'

'*In the Night Garden.*'

'I'm sorry. I've no idea what that is.'

'Of course not. You don't have children, do you?'

'No.'

'*In the Night Garden* is a children's television programme of, to my mind, excessive sentimentality.'

'Ah.'

'Replacing the lead I was following with it was an act of sheer insolence. It was the kidnappers cocking a snook at me.'

'I'm sorry.'

'Not as sorry as I am, Truffler. The thought of letting Mrs Pargeter down is more than I can bear.'

'She'll be very sympathetic.'

'I don't want her sympathy. I want to be able to provide her with the service which she expects from me.'

'Yes, I can see that.'

'It makes me seriously worry about whether I'm losing my touch.'

'No way, Napper.'

But the PR man sounded unsure, his almost bombastic confidence draining out of him like air from a punctured balloon.

Truffler, who had never before been confronted by a moment of doubt from Napper Johnson, tried to reassure him. 'I'm sure someone like you will have other ways of finding out where old Holy Smirke is being held.'

'Of course I do, but they're all more time-consuming than the CCTV method.' Napper spoke more urgently, as if to dismiss his moment of vulnerability. 'Needless to say, I've checked the registration number of the Toyota Prius in which the vicar was abducted. And, needless to say, the car had false plates whose numbers do not appear on the DVLA computer system. I have alerted my network of informants about the kidnap, and they are doing their best, but it's a slow process.'

'Hm. Do you want me to tell all this to Mrs Pargeter?'

'No, no, please don't, Truffler! If failure has to be admitted I would rather deliver the bad news myself. But give me a bit longer. If I've made no more progress by the end of tomorrow, Monday, I will ring Mrs Pargeter and tell her of my inadequacy.'

'Very well. I won't say anything to her till then.'

'Thank you.'

'By the way, Napper, are you having one of your nice country house weekends?'

'I certainly am not! I've given all that up. Since my wife . . .' He still couldn't spell out the words. 'I don't get the pleasure I used to from such occasions, and my hosts and hostesses keep trying to set me up with unattached women. It's very tiring.'

'So what are you up to this weekend?'

'I am personally scouring South London for any trace of a kidnapped vicar.'

Truffler Mason was not the only one to get bad news by phone that Sunday.

Back at Greene's Hotel Mrs Pargeter had woken round eleven with a considerable headache, which was alleviated by the large brunch in a private room which she had ordered for the morning after the hen party.

Sammy and her guests appeared at various times and in various degrees of wanness, but they all perked up with the champagne and breakfast buffet. The old adage that 'nothing is better for a hangover than a big fry-up' was put to the test and proved to be very accurate. Plates piled high with bacon, sausages, black pudding, scrambled eggs, hash browns, tomatoes, mushrooms and baked beans were voraciously wolfed down by the girls. As their heads cleared, so the noise level increased while they giggled their way through reconstructing the antics of the night before.

It was about three o'clock when they all parted in the Greene's Hotel foyer. Mrs Pargeter saw Hedgeclipper Clinton wince behind his counter at the high giggle level, and she grinned across at him. There were then lots of hugs and thank-yous as she said goodbye to the girls. Sammy Pinkerton gave her a particularly big hug and thank-you. 'None of this would have happened without you.'

'Don't worry,' said Mrs Pargeter. 'I loved every minute of it.'

'I'll see you soon.'

'I'll see you tomorrow, actually.'

'Oh?'

'Come on, Sammy, don't be dozy. That's the day you and Kelvin are going to inspect Girdstone Manor.'

'Of course.'

'Gary and I will pick you up at your flat in Southend at ten thirty.'

'Great. We'll be there.'

The Bentley was waiting outside Greene's, and as Gary drove her back to Chigwell Mrs Pargeter felt very pleased with the way the hen party had gone. She rewarded herself with a very comforting little zizz in the car.

The first bad-news call came at about six from Erin. The girl told Mrs Pargeter exactly what she had found – or rather not found – when she got back home.

Erin tried not to allow any emotion into her voice as she spelled out what was missing. She was certainly not about to succumb to tears, but Mrs Pargeter could feel the seething anger behind her impassivity.

'Don't worry,' Mrs Pargeter said. 'We'll find your stuff. And I'm sure some of it is duplicated in Truffler's office. We'll get him on the case.'

'I don't think that'll help much,' said Erin flatly. 'I've just heard from Truffler.' And she told Mrs Pargeter the second tale of woe.

'It must be the same person behind both robberies, Erin, mustn't it?'

'I think it must be.'

'We'll track them down,' said Mrs Pargeter with more confidence than she felt.

'And when we do,' said Erin, her anger spilling over, 'I will personally kill them.'

* * *

The second call of the evening was even more distressing. This time the caller was in tears. It was Sammy.

'What on earth's the matter? Are you just feeling down after the excitement of last night?'

'No, it's nothing to do with that,' Sammy sobbed. 'Last night's about the happiest I've ever been in my life. But when I got back home . . .' Tears stopped further words from coming out.

'Oh Gawd,' said Mrs Pargeter. 'You haven't been burgled, have you?'

'No. Why would you think that?'

'Never mind, love. What has happened?'

'It's much worse than burglary. It's about Kelvin.'

'Is he all right? Has something happened to him?'

'I don't know. I don't know where he is! He's not at the flat.'

'I'm sure he'll turn up.'

'More to the point, he hasn't been to the flat.'

'What do you mean?'

'There's an old girl lives in the ground-floor flat right underneath ours. She's nosy as hell, and she doesn't sleep very well. Always complaining about the noise if one or other of us doesn't get back till after midnight. Well, she told me that Kelvin went out about eight o'clock yesterday evening and . . . he hasn't come back since!' Again the girl was overcome by floods of tears.

'Sammy, I'm sure there's a perfectly logical explanation for—'

'I'm sure there isn't. There's only one explanation that makes any sense – and the sense it makes isn't very nice.'

'You've tried ringing him?'

'Of course I have – ringing, texting, emailing. He seems to have his phone switched off.'

'Well, maybe there's a job he had to do that took longer than—'

'Mrs Pargeter, when I asked Kelvin yesterday what he was going to do while I was at the hen party, he said he was going to stay in the flat, watch some telly, have an early night.'

'Something must have made him change his mind. It needn't be anything sinister. He just—'

'Mrs Pargeter, it's very sweet of you to speak up for him, but we both know what's really happened.'

'Do we?'

'Of course we do. Kelvin spent last night with another woman.'

'You don't know that. There are any number of other explanations for—'

'I know that's what's happened. Before he met me, Kelvin was a bit of a Jack the Lad, popping in and out of any number of girls' beds. So suddenly he gets the opportunity of a night on his own, with me safely in Greene's Hotel, and what does he do? He immediately goes back to bed with one of his old girlfriends.'

'You don't know that.'

'I do! I am absolutely certain of it.'

'Sammy,' said Mrs Pargeter soothingly, 'Kelvin will come back soon with a perfectly sensible explanation for what he's been doing, you'll make up, and we'll go to Girdstone Manor tomorrow to—'

'We will not be going to Girdstone Manor tomorrow or any other day! I'm sorry to have to tell you this, Mrs Pargeter – particularly when you've been so generous to me – but my engagement to Kelvin Stockett is off!'

SEVENTEEN

M rs Pargeter woke on the Monday morning feeling uncharacteristically low. She seemed to be getting nowhere on the case, and then she'd had that upsetting call from Sammy the evening before. Things didn't look good.

She glanced ruefully at the photograph on her bedside table. The very correct Mr Pargeter looked back at her. 'God,' she said, 'I wish you were still around, so's I could pick your brains on this one.'

Partially restored by some toast, marmalade and very strong instant coffee, at ten o'clock sharp she rang the number of Girdstone Manor and once again got through to the snooty Bookings Manager Shereen.

'I'm afraid I'm going to have to postpone the inspection meeting we'd arranged for today. The young man, Kelvin, has a business commitment, which means he can't make it.'

'Are you sure that doesn't mean he's getting cold feet about the whole wedding thing?' Shereen's response was shrewd; she'd clearly been through every emotional ripple of many engagements.

'Good heavens, no,' Mrs Pargeter replied breezily. 'They're both as keen as ever. I'll talk to them and get back to you to fix another date for what we were hoping to do today.'

'Very well,' said Shereen, though there was still an edge of suspicion in her voice. 'And I should remind you, Mrs Pargeter, that since it was last Wednesday when you made the booking, cancellation now will involve the loss of your deposit, and if you cancel any time after this coming Saturday you will, under the terms of our contract, be liable for the full costs of the wedding.'

'I am fully aware of the terms of the contract, Shereen. But have no worries on that score. Samantha Pinkerton and Kelvin Stockett will get married at Girdstone Manor on the twenty-seventh of May!'

Confident and forceful though she sounded, Mrs Pargeter hoped to God that what she was saying was true. Though so well endowed by the late Mr Pargeter that she could pay for a hundred weddings without batting an eyelid, his widow was never profligate with her money. She believed in getting value for it, and so was very determined that the prophecy she had just made to the Girdstone Manor Bookings Manager would come true. Mrs Pargeter had set herself a challenge.

Next, she rang Sammy. 'Are you feeling any better this morning, love? Have you changed your mind?'

'About the wedding? Certainly not!'

'But have you heard anything from Kelvin?'

'Yes, he finally turned up yesterday evening.'

'And?'

'And nothing has changed. I slept on the sofa in the living room. Our engagement is off.'

'So he didn't tell you where he had been on Saturday night?'

'No.'

'Did you mention your thought that he might have been with another woman?'

'Of course I did.'

'And did he deny it?'

'Of course he did.'

'But did he provide any other explanation?'

'No. He just had the nerve to say it was nothing I need worry about.'

'Sammy . . .' Mrs Pargeter chose her words with some delicacy. 'Given Kelvin's somewhat unusual profession . . . do you think it possible that he was out, as it were, on business?'

'You mean: was he committing a burglary?'

'That's exactly what I mean.'

'I suggested that. He denied it. And I didn't see any stuff.'

'"Stuff"?'

'Normally, when Kelvin has committed a burglary he brings the stuff he's stolen back here . . . just for a few days. Until he sells it on to a fence he knows. I hate him doing that. I say it's putting us into unnecessary danger; not that that stops him. But he didn't bring anything home last night.'

'How did he seem in himself? Cheerful? Cocky?'

'Certainly not. He was very twitchy and upset.'

'After you'd told him the engagement was off?'

'Well, he was worse then, but he was twitchy and upset when he arrived. Like he was suffering from shock or something.'

'Did you ask for an explanation of why he was in such a state?'

'I did. And once again he refused to tell me anything.' Sammy started to sob. 'We used to tell each other everything, Mrs Pargeter. Now Kelvin just won't communicate with me at all.'

'Give me his mobile number. I'll try to talk to him.'

'I very much doubt if he'll answer it.' But Sammy gave the number. 'He's certainly not taking my calls.'

'Now what are you going to do today? You mustn't just sit around moping.'

'Well, first thing I've got to do,' Sammy wailed, 'is to ring round all my friends from the hen party and tell them the engagement's off.'

'Don't you dare do that,' said Mrs Pargeter in a tone that had to be obeyed. 'Don't talk to any of them until you've heard from me.'

Mrs Pargeter sat in her sitting room, looking for inspiration from the photograph of her late husband on the mantelpiece. He would have known what to do in these circumstances. He knew what to do in all circumstances. Mrs Pargeter tried to project herself inside his brain and join in with his thought processes.

But her concentration kept being broken by the sight of a pink, white and gold china cat encroaching on her peripheral vision, and she became distracted by trying to think of ways of getting rid of the thing without offending Gary. Her cleaning lady had gone all self-righteous on her when she'd suggested the staging of an accident, so another disposal method would have to be found.

To get away from the cat, Mrs Pargeter went through to the kitchen to make herself a cup of coffee. Though accustomed to the finest Arabica at Greene's Hotel, at home she always made do with instant.

Armed with a cup of strong black, she sat down at the kitchen table and tried to think what to do next.

The events of the weekend had changed almost every aspect of the case and, though Mrs Pargeter was by nature ebulliently optimistic, even she felt a little subdued when she assessed the unknown villains who her team were up against. People who could not only steal all of Erin Jarvis and Truffler Mason's archives, but also hack into Napper Johnson's computer system and make him watch *In the Night Garden* were adversaries who could not be dismissed lightly. Edmund Grainger, she reckoned, must be involved in some way, but she couldn't for the life of her work out how.

The lines around the violet eyes scrunched up as she focused on her problems. Out of all the possibilities, one thing seemed clear. Every mystery that needed solving went back to the early days of her late husband's business career: to the time when he, Holy Smirke and Tony Hardcastle left school. Tony Hardcastle was mostly likely dead; Holy Smirke was hopefully still alive, but frustratingly unavailable for consultation.

Who else was there whose memory might go so far back as to remember the start-up of Mr Pargeter's business empire?

Suddenly, some words of Truffler Mason's came into her head. 'Worked with your husband pretty much from the start, I think.'

Of course. Mrs Pargeter checked the phone number in the little black book and put through a call to Gizmo Gilbert.

EIGHTEEN

I n the intervening ten days the old man seemed to have
become more skeletal than ever. The decorative condition
of his house hadn't improved in the interim, either. But his
old-fashioned courtesy was still all present and correct.

'Mrs Pargeter, this is a great pleasure for me to see you
again so soon. Tell me, have you had satisfactory experiences
with your "Widow's Comf—" erm, "Zipper Zapper"?'

'I've just used it the once, and it worked a treat, Gizmo. It's
in my handbag as we speak. I never go anywhere without it.'

'Excellent.'

'And I really do think it has commercial possibilities.' Memo
to self: check out start-up company for developing 'The Zipper
Zapper' just as soon as all this Sir Normington Winthrop business is sorted out.

'Oh, well, I hope you're right. Now some tea.'

Just as before, it was all laid out ready for her arrival. The
same silver orb of a teapot, the same Denby ware crockery,
the same 1947 Royal Wedding biscuit tin.

'Trust you've been keeping well,' said Mrs Pargeter as
Gizmo poured out the tea. Once again the rock-like steadiness
of his hand was a tribute to the many hours he had spent in
his workshop.

'Never better,' the old man replied. 'What you did last week
gave the fillip my confidence needed. It encouraged me to
believe that I'm still capable of inventing things with commercial possibilities. And in fact –' he was really excited about
something – 'I've been working on a new invention that I
think could be even better than "The Zipper Zapper".'

'Oh, what is it?'

'Better I show you rather than describe it. When you finish
your tea, you must come through to the workshop and I'll—'

But Mrs Pargeter was already out of her armchair, tea cup

in hand. 'I'll bring this through. Can't wait to see what you've come up with.'

Gizmo Gilbert only demurred slightly out of politeness. He was as eager to show off his new creation as she was to see it.

Into the spotless workshop they went. An untidy array of components and tools lay on part of the work surface where he must have been working till interrupted by Mrs Pargeter's arrival.

'The thing that seems to be all the rage these days is making multifunctional objects. You know, if you have the right applications, you can run entire businesses from a mobile phone or a tablet. And I suppose the first major doubling up of functions was when someone had the idea of combining a mobile with a camera.

'I must say, when that first came out, I couldn't see it. I thought: what's the point of having a camera on your phone? You might just as well have a pasta-making machine attached to your wristwatch.

'Which just goes to show what a dinosaur I was – and still am. I got it all wrong. There's a whole generation now that spend most of their lives photographing each other on their phones. But I still thought the principle was interesting – taking two existing pieces of kit and combining them in a way that's simple and saves space.'

'So what two things have you combined?' asked Mrs Pargeter excitedly.

'Well, you know that lots of people these days are drinking too much?'

'So I've heard, yes.'

'And there's quite a market for personal breathalyser testing kits.'

'I'll take your word for it, Gizmo.'

'And what's wrong with most of them is they're too big. You know, size of a mobile phone. Fine if you test yourself at home before going out to see if you're OK to drive. Not so good, though, if you're at a party with lots of people and want to check out whether you should stop drinking. So . . .' The old man reached down to the work surface and lifted up a very small shiny piece of porcelain. 'Any idea what that is, Mrs Pargeter?'

'It looks like a crown for a tooth.'

'Excellent! Spot on! You have won a coconut at your first attempt! That is exactly what it is – a crown for a tooth. But this is no ordinary crown. Within it I have fitted – by considerable miniaturization – a working personal breathalyser.'

'What, so it'd stay in there all the time and let you know when you're going over the limit on the old booze?'

'Exactly. Where better to fit such a device than in the mouth, the very conduit through which all consumed alcohol passes?'

'Yes, that sounds very clever, but how does the device let you know when you've had enough? 'Cause if a buzzer sounds in your mouth or something, that's going to draw attention to you at a party, isn't it?'

'I agree. And for that reason I have invented a much more subtle device than that.' He picked up a small object that looked like an electronic key fob. 'You carry this in your pocket or handbag. And when you've reached your alcohol limit, it doesn't do anything so crude as buzz. No, it vibrates, thus communicating the information to you without anyone else present being aware of what's going on.'

'It's very clever,' said Mrs Pargeter.

The old man beamed. 'Yes, I'm extremely pleased with it myself. And I wouldn't have embarked on inventing anything new if I hadn't received the boost – both financial and personal – I got from your reaction to "The Widow's Comf—" I mean, "The Zipper Zapper". That gave me so much confidence.'

'Good.' Mrs Pargeter wasn't totally convinced about the commercial possibilities of Gizmo Gilbert's latest invention, but she didn't want to dampen his enthusiasm, so she asked cautiously, 'And have you got a name for it?'

'Yes,' came the proud reply. 'It's called "The Pocket Vibrator".'

'Hm.'

He nodded vigorously. 'Does what it says on the tin.'

'Yes, sure, but I . . . er . . . think it could be another candidate for a change of name, actually, Gizmo.'

They were back in the front room with full tea cups when Mrs Pargeter asked, 'You go back a long way, working with my husband, don't you?'

'Certainly do. I was with him pretty much from the start.'

'Were you at school with him?' she asked eagerly. 'Cheesemongers' Hall?'

'No, I don't go quite that far back.'

'How did you meet?'

'Well, my dad was an electrician, and he always assumed I'd follow him into the business. I started a training course at a local Technology College, but I wasn't a very good student, I'm afraid. The teachers, like, wanted me to follow their curriculum, and I wanted to be experimenting with my own stuff. So I dropped out after a couple of terms – well, "was asked to drop out" might be more accurate. So then, anyway, I go back to working with my father, and that wasn't a big success either.'

'Why not?'

'Same reason. He wanted me to get on with mending fuse boxes, setting up light fittings, rewiring houses that were only one step up from slums, and I . . . well, I was still more interested in trying new things out . . . inventions, I suppose.

'Anyway, one day we get a call that some geezer's got a problem with his hi-fi and needs someone to help him out. Well, my old man can't be bothered with jobs like that, so I end up going out to his place, and I'm expecting, like, another dilapidated East End terrace. But no, it's a really nice house, in one of those squares where the prices have gone through the roof in the last twenty years. But round then everything was very shabby – except this one house. Which I think is odd, because when a house gets tarted up like that the locals get quite shirty. They assume these're posh incomers, so pretty soon any tarted-up house has got graffiti all over it and bricks through a few windows and, you know – "Welcome to the neighbourhood and go back to where you come from!"

'But this one house hasn't been touched, which tells me the owner's got a lot of respect in the area. He's the kind of guy nobody's going to mess with. So I knock on the door – and that's the first time I meet Mr Pargeter.

'One thing I notice about him straight away is that he's only a year or two older than me – if even that much. And, looking round the house, I see he's really done well for himself. The hi-fi system he'd got the problem with, that was state-of-the-art, must have set him back a few grand even then – and we're talking a good few years ago.

'Anyway, I pretty soon see that the problem he's got is with his subwoofer, and it doesn't take me long to sort that out. I was very interested in sound systems back then and had just started to explore what could be done with remote controls. So I set up a remote control for your husband's set-up, and he's tickled pink with it.'

'Yes, he did love his music,' said Mrs Pargeter fondly.

'So, anyway, the two of us get talking about this and that, and he's really interested in the potential of remote controls . . . and wider applications for them beyond tellies and radios and that. And then he sets me, like, a challenge. He says it's just for fun, but he'll pay me a grand if I can invent a remote control that'll work over a distance of two hundred yards.'

'What, to open a door?'

'No, wasn't a door. It was for something else.'

'What?'

'A gun.'

'Oh?'

'Your husband wants me to produce a remote control that will make a gun fire even though the person firing it is two hundred yards away.'

'Ah.'

'Well, obviously, I'm up for the challenge, aren't I? I mean, a grand's a lot of money back then, but apart from the money I'm intrigued, want to know if I can really do this. So I get the gun and—'

'*You* got the gun?'

'No, no, your husband got it . . . Well, no, that's not strictly true. He put me in touch with the man he called his "Armourer", and the Armourer got the gun for me. It was an automatic pistol, actually.'

Mrs Pargeter leant forward excitedly. 'And what was the Armourer's name?'

'"Hair-Trigger" Hardcastle.'

'Was his real first name Tony?'

'I don't know. I never heard him called nothing else but Hair-Trigger.'

'It has to be the same guy!'

Gizmo Gilbert looked at her in some bewilderment. He didn't know what she was getting so excited about.

'Sorry, I interrupted your story,' said Mrs Pargeter contritely. 'What happened about your remote control for the gun?'

'I am glad to say that I managed it perfectly.' He glowed with remembered professional pride. 'Produced exactly what your husband had requested. The only difficult bit, really, was miniaturizing the receptor on the pistol's handle. Remote's no problem at all – just developing the range of existing technology.

'So I make the thing within a week – want to impress your old man with how quick off the mark I am. And when I'm working it, I suddenly realize that making stuff like that is what I want to do for the rest of my life. And everything's fine – well, except for my old man. I'm working hard on my invention when I should be putting extra plug sockets in people's bedrooms or mending old ladies' kettles. So, basically, by the end of the week my dad's booted me out of the business.

'But I don't care, because I'm convinced I have made an invention that really works. So I go back to your old man's house exactly a week later to see if the thing will do the business under test conditions. And we don't do it round there – built-up area and that. Your old man was always very good on the old Health and Safety.'

'Oh, he certainly was.'

'So he drives me to this bit of open ground he knows just on the edge of Epping Forest. And he sets up the gun fixed to a tree and pointing at a target on another tree a good fifty yards away. Then he gets out a tape measure and measures out exactly two hundred yards from the tree with the gun on it. And then he says, "Over to you, Gizmo."

'And that kind of cheers me up. No one's ever called me nothing but my proper name before. Your husband invented my nickname. And when he did that, it gave me a good feeling. So I point my remote at the gun and I give myself a countdown.' The old boy was enjoying his narration. 'Five . . . four . . . three . . . two . . . one . . . I press the button on the remote . . . Bang, pistol fires. Then I stroll back down nonchalantly with your old man to check the damage. Pistol fired perfectly into the bull of the target. I know I'm not really responsible for the positioning of the pistol that got the bullseye, but who cares? I feel great.

'And your husband's well impressed too. He says I done just what he wanted. And he says he really wants to explore further what can be done with technology in his line of business. Then he hands across a brown envelope containing a grand in fifties and offers, like, a monthly retainer for me to come on board and work with him.

'I thought Christmas and my birthday had come at the same time. I was well chuffed. One of the best days of my life – though I was to have a few more good ones when I was working with your old man. He was a diamond, Mr Pargeter, a genuine two-thousand-carat diamond.'

'Thank you,' said Mrs Pargeter, because it seemed the appropriate moment to say it. She could hardly contain her excitement. She had now come closer than ever before to finding out the details of her late husband's early career. And she felt sure that Gizmo Gilbert had more information to give her.

'Tell me,' she asked, 'what happened to Hair-Trigger Hardcastle?'

'He went on working with your husband for a few years, sourcing guns and that kind of stuff whenever they was needed, but then . . . there was a big falling-out.'

'Oh?'

'Turns out Hair-Trigger had a scam going. He was creaming off twenty per cent for himself on every deal he done. Well, when your old man found out, he didn't like that. Always being such an honest man himself, he didn't like to see dishonesty in others.'

Mrs Pargeter nodded agreement. 'So what happened to Hair-Trigger?'

'He must've gone off to do something else. For someone else.'

'But you've no idea what? Or for who?'

Gizmo Gilbert shook his head wearily. 'Not a clue, Mrs Pargeter.'

NINETEEN

She was almost out of the door, saying her goodbyes, when Mrs Pargeter remembered there was something else she needed to ask Gizmo Gilbert. It had been floating around in her subconscious since she'd last met him: the niggling feeling that she'd forgotten something that might be important.

'Betrayal!' she said suddenly.

'I beg your pardon?' said Gizmo Gilbert.

'You talked to me last week about people who betrayed my husband.'

'What, you mean like Hair-Trigger Hardcastle?'

'Yes, that was a kind of betrayal. A betrayal of trust, certainly. But mostly it was just straightforward theft, taking his unauthorized cut out of the gun deals. You mentioned another, more serious betrayal – an undercover cop insinuating himself into my husband's operation.'

Gizmo Gilbert nodded. 'Oh yes, the original cuckoo in the nest.'

'Remind me, what was his name?'

'Magnet Mitchell.'

'And you implied that after he was unmasked, he was killed by some hot-headed younger members of my husband's . . . business?'

'I don't know that for sure.'

'Gizmo, I want you to tell me everything possible that you know about Magnet Mitchell.'

'Certainly, Mrs P. But that might take a while, so do you mind if we sit down again?'

She didn't mind. They sat.

When she left Gizmo Gilbert's house and got into Gary's Skoda Octavia, parked discreetly around the corner, Mrs Pargeter felt for the first time since the investigation had started that she might be getting somewhere.

*   *   *

She was slipping gently into a quiet little nap as they drove along when her phone rang. It was Truffler Mason, and there was an urgency in his lugubrious tones. 'Mrs P, there's just been an attempt to kidnap Lady Winthrop.'

'Really?'

'Yes. Where are you?'

'In Gary's Octavia.'

'Then switch on speakerphone. I want him to hear this too.'

Mrs Pargeter did as she was told, then asked, 'Where did the attempted abduction happen?'

'At her house. Two men burst in. They'd got a car waiting outside.'

'What make?'

'Toyota Prius.'

'Right.'

'Anyway, these two villains got into her house, and they were dragging her down the steps to the car when something extraordinarily rare happened.'

'What was it?'

'You'll never believe this. When they get out on to the pavement, the villains see, walking towards them . . . two uniformed coppers.'

'Good grief.'

'Yes, that is a rare moment, isn't it? Policemen appearing actually when they are needed. Like back in the days of having a friendly bobby on the beat. Anyway, the boys in blue see there's someone being abducted, so they run forward, whipping out their walkie-talkies. And the villains are suddenly not so interested in kidnapping Lady Winthrop. They drop her on the pavement, leap into the Prius and depart in an eco-friendly screech of tyres.'

'Is Helena all right?'

'She'll be fine. A bit shaken, but who can blame her? I've spoken to Napper Johnson about her.'

'Oh?'

'Bodyguards are another part of his business. He says he's going to put one of his best female operatives on to guard Lady Winthrop twenty-four/seven. Or he may actually do the job himself.'

'Good. I suppose you haven't heard anything from Napper about Holy Smirke?'

'Mrs Pargeter,' said Truffler Mason, a little reproachfully. 'You should know that the minute we get any info there, you will be the first to know.'

'Of course I know that. Bless you, Truffler.'

'Anyway, the reason I want Gary to hear this—'

'Morning, Truffler,' said the chauffeur's voice from the front of the Octavia.

'Morning, Gary. Listen, I want you to take on bodyguard duties for Mrs Pargeter.'

'But I don't need any of that,' she protested. 'I'm in no danger.' Again, stubbornly, she made no mention of the call from Edmund Grainger.

'Mrs P,' said Truffler wearily. 'Holy Smirke got kidnapped because he might have been able to give you information about the early days of Sir Normington Winthrop's career. Lady Winthrop was nearly kidnapped because she's trying to find out details of her husband's early career. You are investigating exactly the same thing. I would say you were definitely at risk from whoever these people are.'

'You might have a point.'

'I *do* have a point, Mrs P. And for that reason I am asking you not to go off on your own making further investigations.'

'Very well,' she said. And then, in a mood of contrition, she finally told them about the call she'd had from Edmund Grainger.

It was the first time she had ever seen Truffler Mason really angry. 'Why the hell didn't you mention that before?'

'I don't know. I just thought he was a bully and I don't like letting bullies win.' Even as she said them she knew how inadequate her words sounded.

With great restraint Truffler curbed his anger. 'Well, that's all the more reason why you need protection,' he said. 'Gary, you keep an eye on her. Don't let her out of your sight.'

'Right you are,' said Gary, who wouldn't find following Truffler's instructions any hardship at all.

Though when she had spoken to Sammy Pinkerton earlier in the day, the girl had said Kelvin wasn't taking her calls, Mrs Pargeter still thought it was worth trying to get through to him. When they had met at Greene's Hotel, she'd had reservations about his choice of career, but the one thing she'd never doubted was the quality of his devotion to Sammy. Every time he'd looked at his fiancée, it was as if he wanted to bundle her up into his arms and protect her from all the evil in the entire world.

Mrs Pargeter therefore conjectured that though he might have reacted initially with pique when Sammy informed him the engagement was off, he would in more thoughtful moments since have been wondering how he could get things back to the happier status quo. And that was one of her goals too.

When she rang, still from the back of the Octavia, Kelvin Stockett sounded very cautious and suspicious, but at least he did answer the phone.

Mrs Pargeter's identification of herself prompted a very terse, 'What do you want?'

'Listen, Kelvin, I've heard from Sammy that the engagement's off.'

'Yes.'

'I was just ringing to say I'm very sorry.'

'I'm not exactly ecstatic about the situation myself.'

'And she's got it wrong, hasn't she? You didn't spend Saturday night with another woman?'

'No, of course I didn't!'

'But you were out all night?'

'Yes.'

'Doing a job for people who've forbidden you to talk about it . . .?' Mrs Pargeter hazarded.

'Yes. Exactly.'

'And why can't you tell Sammy that?'

'Because . . . well, look, you know that she doesn't fully approve of my profession?'

'I had pieced that together, yes.'

'And anyway, I did lie to her about Saturday. I told her I'd just watch telly and have an early night, but even as I was saying the words I knew I was going to be off on this big job all night. I lied to her. I was out doing a burglary.'

'I think she'd much rather you were doing that than being in bed with another woman.'

'Maybe, but I still lied to her.'

'Kelvin, you want Sammy back, don't you? You still want to marry her?'

'More than I've ever wanted anything in my entire life.'

'Then we need to meet.'

Kelvin had suggested the Greyhound, the pub near the flat he shared – or possibly had shared – with Sammy. Their local – or what had been their local. The thought that their relationship might be over hurt Kelvin like a physical pain. That's why he'd so readily agreed to meet Mrs Pargeter. She had the air about her of someone who would get things done.

Mrs Pargeter herself was delighted by the venue. From when she was a child, growing up in the area, she had always loved Southend. Also, it was getting near lunchtime, and Mrs Pargeter always associated Southend with fish and chips.

Gary's Skoda Octavia did not look conspicuous in the car park of the Greyhound. The other cars were from a similar price range, and there were a couple of white vans. Just as well he hadn't driven the Bentley.

Gary, mindful of Truffler's instructions, insisted on coming into the pub too, but Mrs Pargeter insisted that he should not look as if he was with her. So they gave the impression once inside the pub that they had never met before but had just happened to arrive at the door at the same time.

Kelvin was already sitting at a table in the corner, two-thirds of the way down a pint of lager. His face suggested that the horse on which he had staked his entire month's salary had just limped in a resounding last. Which actually wasn't a bad metaphor for what had happened to him.

He looked up at Mrs Pargeter's entrance, recognizing her at once. (Nobody who'd met her once ever failed to recognize her again.)

'Hello, Kelvin,' she said breezily. She pointed to his glass. 'Looks like you need a top-up. What is it?'

'San Miguel.'

'Because I'm in Southend and because it's lunchtime I'm going to order fish and chips. Same for you?'

'I don't feel much like eating at the moment.'

'I'll order you fish and chips.' She strode across to the bar, ordered a pint of San Miguel and, for herself, a Vodka Campari. 'I'll move on to the wine later,' she said to the cheery young barman. 'And fish and chips twice, please. Can I put that on a tab?'

No problem. As she moved across to join Kelvin she noticed that Gary had retired to a table on the other side of the bar, from which she would always be in his eyeline. He'd picked up a copy of the *Sun* from the bar and was perusing it as he sipped at a glass of mineral water. Gary was always very good about not drinking when he was working. Losing a licence could all too easily finish off a car-hire business like his.

'Well, look,' said Mrs Pargeter, after she had raised the Vodka Campari to the doom-struck young man sitting opposite her, 'I know you're afraid the whole relationship's over, but I think things can be sorted out between you.'

'No, they can't,' he said despondently. 'What happened at the weekend wasn't really the cause of Sammy breaking off the engagement. It was, if you like, a symptom of what has been going wrong for some time.'

'I'm sorry.'

'And, in fact, what you said on the phone, about her preferring me to be off working than with another woman? That might not actually be true.'

'You mean it's basically your profession that's driving a wedge between the two of you?'

He nodded miserably, like a dog that's just been refused a walk.

'Is Sammy worried about you being caught and arrested?'

Kelvin dismissed the suggestion with something approaching contempt. 'She knows I'm too good at it for that to happen.'

'So it's a moral issue?'

'I guess so. Sammy thinks it's wrong to take other people's stuff.' There was a note of bewilderment in his voice at the incongruity of this idea.

'Well,' said Mrs Pargeter gently, 'a lot of people would agree with her there.'

'But I keep telling her . . . when I steal from individuals

it's only stuff they can easily get replaced by their insurance. And when I steal from commercial companies, the damage I do is so minimal that they're often not even aware of it.' He was careful not to mention what he'd been doing at the weekend, which didn't fit into either of these categories.

'"Victimless crimes", eh?'

'Pretty much.'

Mrs Pargeter did not pass judgement on his reply. Instead, she said, 'And you're doing this – you've chosen this route through life – because of your father?'

'Yes, I'd like to do something to make him proud of me. I was never able to achieve that while I was alive, because my mother tried to stop us from having any kind of relationship, but I want to make up for that.'

'And do you think he would be proud of you now?'

A glow of self-esteem burst through the young man's misery. 'I think he would. I've worked so hard to try to emulate him. And I am now – I can say without any false modesty – one of the best burglars in the country.'

'Congratulations,' said Mrs Pargeter drily. 'How much do you know about your father's career?'

'Apart from the fact that he was a burglar, and he died in a motorcycle accident, not a lot. As I said, my mother did everything possible to keep us apart.'

'Even, I've heard, to the extent of giving you her surname rather than his.'

'Yes. By the time I realized what had happened, the name "Kelvin Stockett" was on so many forms, school registers and so on, that it was too late to do anything about it.'

'But you do know what your father's surname was?'

'Of course I do. It was Mitchell.'

'And do you know what he was called by his professional associates?'

'Yes. Magnet Mitchell.'

'This morning I've found out rather a lot about the career of Magnet Mitchell.'

'Have you?' Kelvin sounded really excited. 'How did you find it out?'

'Well, normally I would have used the archival services of

two experts I know – Truffler Mason and Erin Jarvis.' Mrs Pargeter was not expecting any reaction to the names, so didn't notice the tremor of recognition that crossed Kelvin Stockett's face. 'But their records are . . . currently unavailable, so I consulted another of your father's former colleagues.'

'This is wonderful, Mrs Pargeter. I've been starved of information about my old man all my life, so please tell me everything you know.'

'Very well. I will.'

And she proceeded to tell him everything that she had learned from Gizmo Gilbert. How Magnet Mitchell had developed his skills as a burglar in order to become accepted as one of the team on the late Mr Pargeter's payroll. But how all the time he had actually been in the employ of the Metropolitan Police, awaiting the moment when he showed his true colours and shopped the lot of them to the authorities.

When she finished there was a silence.

'So,' Mrs Pargeter continued after a while, 'it looks like you've been following the wrong role model, Kelvin.'

'Yes,' he murmured, still stunned, still trying to take in all this new information.

'Your father's cover was so deep that he couldn't even tell his wife that he was actually working for the Met. She, daughter of a Chief Constable, despised him all his life for being a burglar, while he was actually on her side.'

There was a shocked silence from Kelvin. Then, suddenly, he stood up and announced, 'I must join the police force as soon as possible!'

TWENTY

I t was a Council of War. 'Just like the old days,' said Gary, rubbing his hands together with relish. Then he noticed he was receiving a rather old-fashioned look from Mrs Pargeter, so he stopped rubbing his hands together with relish.

They were in a private room at Greene's Hotel. Mrs Pargeter, Gary, Truffler, Napper Johnson and Erin Jarvis. And though the atmosphere hadn't quite got to the level of an interrogation, Kelvin Stockett – or Kelvin Mitchell, as he now wished to be called – was enduring fairly tough questioning.

But now his ambitions had shifted from crime perpetration to crime prevention he was an extremely useful witness. Truffler Mason and Erin Jarvis were both hugely relieved when he revealed himself to be the perpetrator of the thefts from their offices. He had transferred all their belongings to the back room of the house off Lavender Hill, and when he'd last been there in the early hours of Sunday morning everything had looked intact.

'I still don't really see,' said Erin, 'why they wanted our stuff.'

Mrs Pargeter explained. 'They want to do anything that will stop us making any progress in our investigation of Sir Normington Winthrop's background. That's why they kidnapped Holy Smirke, so that he couldn't talk to us. It's why they set up Kelvin to rob your office – and Truffler's. That's why they tried to kidnap Helena Winthrop – because they knew she'd contacted Truffler and been in touch with me.'

She looked across to the immaculately-suited Napper Johnson. 'How is Helena, by the way? Not too traumatized by her recent experiences?'

'She's a wonderfully resilient woman,' he replied, his smiling face tinged with something like a blush. 'Obviously, so far I have only had a brief meeting with her, but I get the feeling she is going to be a very congenial person to keep under protection.'

'Good,' said Mrs Pargeter with an answering grin. Then she turned back to Kelvin. 'And while you were transferring Truffler and Erin's stuff, did you get a chance to see much of the rest of the house?'

'Not really. It was just in the front door, through the hall to the back room. Time and again until I'd got it all stowed.'

'And you say you were set up for the job by Edmund Grainger?'

'That's what he called himself. And he was certainly the guy in the photograph Truffler showed me.'

'And was he in the house on the Saturday night when you delivered the stuff?'

'No.'

'So who was there?'

'Couple of heavies.'

Truffler Mason thrust across a still taken from the CCTV footage of Holy Smirke being abducted from in front of St-Crispin-in-the-Closet. 'Those two?'

Kelvin screwed up his eyes. 'Could be. They were about the same size, but I didn't really get a good look at them.'

'And in the house,' Mrs Pargeter said, pressing on, 'did you hear any sounds?'

'What kind of sounds?'

'Well, human sounds. I mean, was there anyone else in the house?'

'I don't think so.'

'Why, what were you thinking, Mrs Pargeter?' asked Napper Johnson.

'Just that if they've got this house down there, *south of the river*, they might use it as a storage space for other things apart from stolen archives.'

'Human things, you were thinking?'

'It's a possibility.'

'Like a kidnapped vicar?' Napper suggested.

'It's a thought.'

'It certainly is.'

'Right,' said Gary, who was getting a bit bored with all this talk and wanted some action. 'When are we going to break into this place?'

'I think tomorrow morning would be favourite,' said Truffler.

'Dawn raid?' asked Gary excitedly.

'Dawn raid,' Truffler confirmed.

'Just like the old days.' Gary chuckled with satisfaction.

Mrs Pargeter looked serenely bewildered by his words.

'First thing is,' said Truffler Mason, spreading a large scale map of Battersea across the table, 'to work out what we're up against.'

'How d'you mean?' asked Erin.

'Well, Kelvin only saw two blokes, but there may be more of them. Edmund Grainger might be back there. We don't know. Also, though we're hoping to surprise them, they seem like quite an efficient line-up. And we don't know whether they're armed or not. Did you see any weapons, Kelvin?'

'No.'

'But that doesn't mean they don't have any. And from the impressions I've got of the kind of villains they are, I think they probably will be tooled-up. Better have the shooters, Gary.'

The chauffeur nodded, making a mental note of the instruction. 'What do you reckon about cars, Truffler?'

'Think we might need two. Those terraces have got little gardens or yards round the back. We'll need to cut off the escape route that way.'

'OK. Well, I'll drive one, anyway. And I suppose I could get one of my drivers to—'

'No, Gary. We don't want to let anyone new in on this. Security risk.'

'I could drive the other car,' suggested Kelvin.

Truffler looked at the young man for a moment, then said, 'Yes, why not?' Then he had second thoughts. 'Just a minute, though.' He looked around the group. 'Saturday night this Herbert was cleaning out my office, not to mention Erin's place. He's changed sides rather quickly, hasn't he?'

'I will vouch for him,' said Mrs Pargeter. And that was that.

Truffler looked at his watch. 'Schedule's pretty tight because we haven't cased the joint properly yet. We'd better get on with that as soon as possible.'

'Do we really need to do that?' asked Gary. 'I mean, Kelvin's already been inside the place.'

'Yes, but you know how insistent Mr Pargeter always was about preparation for a job.'

'But there's other ways of doing that kind of stuff today.'

'Is there?' Truffler didn't like the direction in which the conversation was going. He was a traditionalist. He reckoned that if the late Mr Pargeter had a way of doing something then that was the way it should still be done.

'Erin'll show you, Truffler,' said Gary.

On cue, the girl started flicking her fingers over the screen of her tablet. 'We can check the place out on Google Maps.'

This they did, though Truffler didn't think it was as good as doing a proper recce. He expressed his displeasure by taking copious longhand notes on the positions of doors, windows and other possible emergency exits.

When that was done he said, 'Right. Let's think what else we need. Getting into the place . . . They're going to have pretty substantial security locks. Pity we haven't got time to bring in old "Keyhole" Crabbe. He's the master with the picklocks and that. He's—'

'Excuse me,' Kelvin interrupted. 'I can deal with any locks we're going to come up against. Back in the days when I was a burglar . . .' In other words, yesterday, thought Mrs Pargeter '. . . I taught myself the lot. And I did notice the kind of locks they'd got on the front door when I was carrying all the stuff in. Kid's stuff. I could crack those with a bent hairpin.'

'Good. So let's just confirm who's on the team. How many of us are there going to be? You up for it, Napper?'

'Well, normally I'd say a very definite yes. But in this case I am a little worried about the safety of Lady Winthrop. One of my junior staff is protecting her at the moment, but I feel this is a job that I should really take on personally, given the level of jeopardy she is in.'

Mrs Pargeter raised an eyebrow, but made no comment. Napper went on, 'In fact, I think I should be getting back to her right now. My junior staff are good, but not that good.' He looked round at the assembled plotters. 'Good luck with the dawn raid.' And he left.

Mrs Pargeter had a moment of disquiet. This was only the second time she'd met Napper Johnson, but from what she'd heard about him from Truffler his withdrawal from the proposed raid seemed out of character. She felt a momentary twinge of suspicion. Was Napper on their side or not?

But Truffler showed no signs of anxiety as he continued the planning meeting. He looked across at the chauffeur. 'You're in obviously. And if things get dodgy we might be glad of your getaway skills, Gary.'

'Always at your service.'

'Now, Kelvin, you're in, aren't you? You're going to be very useful to us because you know the place . . .'

'Ye-es.' The young man looked confused.

'What's your problem?'

'Well, the thing is, having so recently decided to give up burglary, I'm wondering whether I should be immediately involving myself in what, when you come down to it, is just another burglary.'

'This is not a burglary,' said Truffler patiently. 'It is a reacquisition of stolen property.'

'Oh, that's all right then,' said Kelvin. 'I'm in.'

'And I'm obviously in.' Truffler let out a sound that could have been a laugh or a groan. 'Apart from anything else, I want to reclaim the contents of the Mason De Vere Detective Agency.'

'And I want to be there for the same reason: to get my stuff,' said Erin Jarvis.

Gary disagreed. 'It might be risky, Erin. If the shooters come out, you could get hurt. You wait till we've made the place safe, then you can come in and collect your stuff.'

'I want to be there,' the girl reiterated with such force that no one argued with her any further.

Truffler Mason looked across at Mrs Pargeter and said slowly, 'I'm afraid I don't think you should be there, Mrs P.'

'Why? I'm not afraid of—'

'I know you're not afraid of nothing. But the fact is that, though we know what we're doing is entirely kosher, there are some people who might regard breaking into a house as an act of burglary.'

'What kind of people?'

'The police, for instance. We're good, we won't make much noise, but in a suburban area like that, there's always the danger that some Neighbourhood Watch nut sees something suspicious and summons the boys in blue. I wouldn't like you to be caught in circumstances like that, Mrs P. I would hate for your name ever to be associated with something that could be interpreted as criminal.'

She was disappointed, but she knew that Truffler was speaking good sense.

'We'll report back to you the minute the job's done,' he reassured her.

'You do that,' she said. 'Doesn't matter how early. You call me as soon as you're safely inside.'

'Of course I will.'

She thought it was worth one more try. 'I'd really like actually to be there, though.'

'No,' Truffler said firmly. 'It is very important that you're *not* there for the raid. What you don't see, Mrs P, you don't know about.'

'Ooh,' she said. 'You sounded just like my husband then.'

Mrs Pargeter had decided she would spend the night at Greene's Hotel. Hedgeclipper Clinton kept a suite ready for her at all times. So after saying goodbye to the others in the foyer, she took Kelvin by the hand and led him through to the bar. 'Someone I want you to see,' she whispered.

Inside the lighting was subdued, most of it coming from low candles on the tables. 1930s jazz murmured from the speakers. Sammy Pinkerton, a champagne bottle in a bucket on a stand beside her, looked fabulous in the candlelight. It airbrushed away the redness that was still around her eyes and picked up the sheen of her black hair, at the same time finding the sparkles of her champagne glass. A matching glass stood empty at the place opposite her.

She didn't look directly at her former fiancé, but addressed Mrs Pargeter. 'Is it true?'

'Yes,' came the comforting reply. 'He's given up crime completely.'

'I'm going to become a cop,' said Kelvin.

Sammy looked at him in amazement, then turned to Mrs Pargeter for elucidation.

'No worries, love. Take it slowly. Kelvin's got a lot to tell you.' Mrs Pargeter took the champagne out of its bucket and filled the empty glass. She gestured Kelvin to sit down in front of it. Which, awkwardly, he did.

'What's going on?' asked Sammy, on the edge of bewildered tears.

'Kelvin'll tell you.' As she spoke, Mrs Pargeter put down on the table between them the key to another of Greene's Hotel's luxury suites. 'You won't want to be going all the way out to Essex at this time of night.'

'What's going on?' Sammy asked again, a little plaintively.

'What's going on,' Mrs Pargeter replied, 'is that you and Kelvin are going to get married at Girdstone Manor on the twenty-seventh of May. One small change, Sammy. You won't be becoming "Mrs Stockett". You'll be becoming "Mrs Mitchell".'

'What?'

But there was no answer to Sammy's question. Mrs Pargeter was already on her way to her suite, feeling rather better at the end of the day than she had at the beginning.

TWENTY-ONE

The dawn raid, when it happened, was a bit of a damp squib. Not in the sense that it wasn't successful – nobody could ever have asked for a smoother job – but the level of opposition for which they had prepared did not materialize. They certainly didn't need to use the guns which Gary had produced from the glove compartments of his black 4 x 4. (He was always very thoughtful about which vehicle he used for which job, and he'd never thought the Bentley would be suitable for a dawn raid. Much better something with all-terrain possibilities.)

The dawn raiders had met at four thirty outside Truffler Mason's office and driven in convoy to Lavender Hill. Kelvin, knowing all too well how much clobber he would have to shift back to where he had stolen it from, had got one of Gary's team to deliver a Transit for him to Greene's Hotel at four o'clock. (He'd snuck out of his suite, leaving Sammy deeply asleep, with everything once more wonderful between them.) He'd driven Erin to Battersea while Truffler went with Gary.

When they got to the target house the Transit was parked round the back, while Gary stopped the 4 x 4 directly in front. Then Kelvin walked round to work wonders with his picklocks.

The front door gave inwards and, cautiously, guns at the ready, Truffler, Gary and Kelvin entered the hall. But the anticipated firefight did not ensue.

In fact, what happened was the one thing they hadn't planned for. They met no resistance at all. The two heavies Kelvin had met on the Saturday night appeared blearily at the foot of the stairs and, seeing three armed men in front of them, immediately ran towards the back of the house and access to the garden.

From inside the Transit van, Erin Jarvis saw them flinging

themselves over the garden wall and running away as fast as they could go. There was nothing she could do to stop them.

(In fact, when he later wrote up a report on the incident, Truffler Mason had a lot of criticisms to make. Their planning of the dawn raid had been seriously inadequate. If the two heavies had come at them with guns, the outcome could have been very different. And what use was Erin going to be sitting in the Transit waiting to cut off any escape out of the back of the house? No, Truffler Mason felt rather bad about how hasty their planning had been. If a similar situation came up again, he would insist that everything was done exactly as the late Mr Pargeter would have done it.)

But the moment that they had broken into the house and seen off its occupants was not the time for recrimination. Kelvin took Truffler to show him where all his precious files were stowed. Then he fetched Erin from round the back to reassure her that her archive was safe too. Both she and Truffler looked delighted to be reunited with their possessions.

And then Kelvin began the laborious process of putting back into the new Transit all of the stuff that he had so painstakingly taken out of the other Transit in the small hours of the Sunday morning. But he didn't make any fuss about the task. He regarded it as a kind of necessary penance – part of the process of transition from lawbreaker to lawkeeper.

The terraced house appeared only to have two stories. There was no obvious access to an attic or cellar. The successful intruders searched all the rooms. Truffler helped himself to a couple of laptops and all the files he could find. 'Tit for tat,' he said. 'If they're going to help themselves to our archive, it's only fair that we should take theirs.'

But they didn't find anything else of particular interest in the house.

They were standing in the empty front room when a very sweaty Kelvin poked his head round the door. 'All done,' he said. 'The Transit's loaded up.'

'Right.' Truffler took out his mobile. 'I'd better just ring Mrs P and tell her everything's OK.'

'Just a minute,' said Erin. 'I can hear a television.'

'What?'

'I can hear a television.'

They were silent for a moment. Truffler, whose hearing wasn't as acute as the girl's, couldn't hear anything. Gary thought he possibly could, but the sound was more likely coming from next door. 'I lived in a terrace once. You could hear the neighbours changing their minds.'

'No, listen again,' said Erin.

Once again they were silent. Then Erin said, 'It's coming from downstairs. Definitely. There's someone down there.'

They made another, more meticulous, examination of the ground floor. Truffler moved along the walls of the hall, rapping on them with his knuckles. It didn't take long. While most of his taps produced a dull thud of flesh against brickwork, there was one whole panel that echoed the space behind it.

Gary and Kelvin helped as they tried to shift the blockage. At first nothing happened. Then Truffler had the idea of lifting the panel slightly. Instantly, it came free. They slid it along the wall to reveal the staircase leading down. The door at cellar level was locked, but Kelvin's instruments made sure it didn't stay that way for long.

He pushed the door open to reveal a very grumpy-looking chubby man in a cassock.

'Don't worry,' said Truffler. 'We're not going to hurt you. We're all friends of Mrs Pargeter.'

'Thank God for that,' said Holy Smirke. 'I knew you'd come eventually.'

'How did you know?'

The vicar pointed upwards. 'Well, obviously, I prayed for it, didn't I?' He looked up at the ceiling. 'Mind you, you took your time answering my prayer, didn't you, God?'

'Are you all right?' asked Gary.

'Well, I'm as all right as anyone can be when they've been locked in a cellar for the best part of a week.'

'Did they hurt you?'

'Not physically, no.'

Truffler was instantly alert. 'What, you mean they hurt you mentally? Brainwashed you?'

'No, no, no. It was almost as bad, though. They just left me in this room with only that telly for company.' He gestured towards it disparagingly. 'Have you any idea how terrible daytime television is?'

TWENTY-TWO

Mrs Pargeter was immediately rung with the happy news of Holy Smirke's rescue, and she undertook to pass it on to the anxious Ernestine in the flat behind St-Crispin-in-the-Closet.

Thereafter it seemed logical that the liberated vicar should be taken straight to Greene's Hotel, and once there it seemed logical that he and the rescue party should join Mrs Pargeter for the delights of the full English breakfast (in a private room, rather than the decorous bustle of the breakfast buffet with other guests). The only one not to take his place at the table with them was Kelvin Mitchell (as he now insisted on being called). He returned to the suite he'd left so early in the morning to enjoy the warm delights of Sammy and room service.

So the group in the private room comprised Mrs Pargeter, Truffler Mason, Gary and Erin, all breathlessly gathered round Holy Smirke, waiting to hear what revelations he had for them.

'First things first,' said Mrs Pargeter, once they had all given their orders and were supplied with coffee. 'We want to know who was behind your kidnapping, Holy. Do you have the photograph, Truffler?' The private investigator proffered the sheet to the vicar. 'Did you have any contact with that man?'

Holy Smirke recognized Edmund Grainger instantly. 'Yes, he interrogated me a few times.'

'He didn't use physical force against you?'

'No, Mrs P. He bullied me and shouted at me and threatened me a bit, but he didn't actually hit me.'

'Good. And what was he interrogating you about? What information was he trying to get from you?'

'It all went back to the early days of your husband starting up his business.'

'I thought it might. The very stuff we want to ask you about, Holy.'

'And the very stuff we would have asked you about if you hadn't been kidnapped,' Truffler added.

'Mind you,' said the vicar with some pride, 'I didn't tell them anything useful.'

'Good for you,' said Mrs Pargeter. 'But I'm afraid I'm going to have to ask you some of the same questions.'

'Hearing them from you will be a pleasure, Mrs Pargeter.'

'Thank you. Now, you and my husband were at school together, weren't you, Holy?'

'Started on the same day at Cheesemongers' First School and then went on to Cheesemongers' Hall together.'

'So you were –' Mrs Pargeter chose the word delicately – 'working with him from the start?'

'Absolutely.' The vicar sighed fondly. 'Happy days.'

At this moment a squad of immaculately uniformed waiters appeared with the customized orders of the breakfast party. A brief interlude of gratified munching ensued.

Then Mrs Pargeter continued her debriefing of Holy Smirke. 'When we last met, I asked you whether back in those days you'd ever come across someone called Normington Winthrop.'

'And I told you then that I hadn't. And were you to ask me again, I'd give you the same answer. His name wasn't mentioned while I was stuck in that hole watching breakfast television.'

'No, but there was a third person from your schooldays who also worked with the two of you, wasn't there? Tony Hardcastle?'

'Oh yes. Hair-Trigger Hardcastle.' Holy Smirke grinned at the recollection. 'Bit of a tearaway, old Hair-Trigger.'

'He was known, too, as the Armourer?'

'Too right. Always had a fascination with guns. More than a healthy fascination with them, I'd say. Hair-Trigger was far too keen on carrying them in the course of ordinary jobs – not afraid of using them either. Your husband kept tearing him off a strip about it, but Hair-Trigger took no notice. Went on his own sweet way. Always tooled-up. I think he was one of those rather pathetic types who didn't feel properly masculine if he wasn't carrying a gun. Thought it gave him an edge with the girls, though from what I could see it didn't seem to. He was an ugly bit of work, and girls used to think that whether he was carrying or not.'

'There was a falling-out between Hair-Trigger and my husband, wasn't there?'

'Yes. I never heard the full details, but I gather Hair-Trigger was cheating your old man out of something – creaming off a bit for himself, I dare say. Also, he had some views on foreigners which would now be called racist, and your husband wasn't keen on that either. So, finally, Mr Pargeter says it has to be a parting of the ways and, ever generous like he was, he gives Hair-Trigger a few grand, like, so he can set up some new business on his own, and that's it. They don't see each other no more.'

'And do you know, Holy, what Hair-Trigger Hardcastle did after that?'

'Not for certain, no. I know what he *wanted* to do after that.'

'Which was?'

'Well, like I said, he was always a loudmouth. Talked himself up a lot, so you had to take everything he said with a skip-load of salt. But I remember being in a boozer with him a few days before the final split with your old man happened, and Hair-Trigger opened up to me a bit about his plans. He reckoned what he was doing, sourcing the odd shooter for minor jobs, was small beer. He had bigger ambitions. What he really wanted to do was get into the international trade.'

'Gun-running?' asked Mrs Pargeter.

'Exactly that. Hair-Trigger said the one market you can always guarantee is the market for weapons. Every day there's a new war – official or unofficial – starting up in some country or other, so the demand's always there. He reckoned he could increase his operation from low-key stuff in the London suburbs to an international business.'

'And do you know if he succeeded in that ambition?'

'Haven't a clue. I'd have thought if he had made it big, we'd have heard more about him. And till you mentioned him just now, I haven't heard his name for getting on for twenty years.'

'And what was the last thing you heard about him back then?'

'I heard he'd gone off to try his luck gun-running in Africa.'

'In Africa? Whereabouts?'

'The Congo.'

TWENTY-THREE

oly Smirke didn't have a lot more information to give, but at least he had opened up a whole new area of investigation. As soon as Truffler Mason and Erin Jarvis had got their archives set up again in their respective offices, there would be lots of lines of research for them to pursue. A rather disgruntled Kelvin Mitchell (he'd been having such a good time in the suite with his fiancée) was summoned to get back in the Transit and return its contents.

The breakfast was drawing to an end. Because of the length of Holy Smirke's debriefing, the meal had taken quite a long time. It was after eleven when Mrs Pargeter received a text on her mobile.

She read it and looked across at Holy, who had eaten hugely and was blissfully mopping up the last juices of tomato and egg with his fried bread. 'Text from Ernestine,' said Mrs Pargeter.

'Oh yes?'

'She wants you back at the flat by one.'

'No problem.'

'Because she's cooking you *pot au feu.*'

'Ah.' His rosy face went a little pale.

'She says she prayed yesterday that you'd be released today, and she knew it'd work so she immediately started cooking the *pot au feu.* It'll be ready at one.'

'Ah,' Holy said again.

'Remind me,' said Mrs Pargeter gently. 'What are the ingredients of a *pot au feu?*'

'Ernestine's special recipe includes a chicken, beef, smoked bacon, Toulouse sausages, carrots, onions, leeks, pepper, garlic, potatoes and a few other secret bits and pieces.'

It was Mrs Pargeter's turn to say, 'Ah.' Then: 'Will you be able to eat all that after the breakfast you've just put away?'

Holy Smirke looked really scared. 'I'll have to,' he replied. 'With Ernestine food is very significant. It's like love. If I don't finish up every mouthful she's served out for me, she thinks I don't love her any more.'

'Good luck,' said Mrs Pargeter.

At the end of their extended breakfast, Mrs Pargeter asked Gary to drive her back to Chigwell. He said the 4 x 4 wasn't really right for that kind of trip and offered to go and get the Bentley. She said he was talking nonsense and she was quite happy in the 4 x 4.

Truffler and Erin said they'd go back to Erin's place in North London, because he wanted to check out the laptop he'd taken from the Lavender Hill house that morning and he knew that she had superior IT skills.

Back in her mansion Mrs Pargeter lay on the sitting room sofa – ensuring, first, that she lay in a position where the china cat was not in her eyeline – and had a doze. The stand-off between her and the figurine had not been helped by the fact that Gary, seeing her into the house earlier in the after-noon, had said, 'Looks great, doesn't it? Like it's always been there.'

It was early evening when she was woken from her zizz by a call from Truffler Mason. 'Hi, Mrs P, I'm over at Erin's, and we've been going through the stuff on the laptop we picked up this morning. A long way to go, but we've already got one lead I just couldn't wait to tell you about.'

'What is it?' she asked eagerly.

'Concerns Hair-Trigger Hardcastle.'

'Oh yes? What, a means of contacting him now?'

'No. If what we've found here is true, Hair-Trigger Hardcastle has been uncontactable for nearly twenty years.'

'You mean he's dead?'

'That's the way it looks. I've found a file of scanned news-paper clippings.'

'And?'

'And they are from some English language paper published in the Congo.'

'Really?' Mrs Pargeter breathed.

'Yes. I think it was printed for expats, but the significant headline reads: "ENGLISHMAN'S BODY FOUND IN JUNGLE – MURDER SUSPECTED." I'll read you the relevant bit.'

There was a silence while Truffler found his place, then he started: 'In the jungle east of Kindu, local hunters made the gruesome discovery of a white man's body. Though it was in an advanced state of decay and partly eaten away by predators, a passport and other papers confirm that the dead man's name was Anthony Hardcastle. He appeared to have been shot through the head. Unsubstantiated rumours suggest that Hardcastle had been involved in the supply of Russian-made weapons to guerrilla groups in the area. He was last seen in Kindu two months ago in the company of a man identified locally as "Mr Winthrop", who is also believed to have been involved in the illegal trafficking of weapons. Mr Winthrop appears to have moved out of his house in Kindu and has not been seen in the area for some time.'

'It has to be the same Mr Winthrop, doesn't it?' Mrs Pargeter bubbled with excitement.

'Certainly a big coincidence if it isn't. Given where the laptop was found.'

'And from the way the report's written, the inference must be that it was Normington Winthrop who killed Hair-Trigger Hardcastle.'

'Certainly looks that way,' Truffler agreed.

'I'm surprised newspapers are allowed to make accusations like that.'

'Ah, Mrs Pargeter, you have grown up in a country where, despite frequent abuses against it, the principle is still maintained of someone being innocent until proven guilty. Other countries are not such sticklers for that kind of approach. And I wouldn't have thought journalistic standards are of the highest in an English-language rag for expats in the middle of the Congo.'

'No, you could be right. But this is brilliant, Truffler! We have finally got something that connects Normington Winthrop with someone who worked for my husband. Which means we're closer to finding out why Normington Winthrop's name was in the little black book.'

'Yes. Mind you, it's a long time ago. Be difficult to investigate further without going out to the Congo, and even then it'd be tricky. People's memories are short.'

'Oh, don't be so defeatist, Truffler. I'm sure there's stuff we can find out in this country.'

'Well, good luck.' He sounded even more lugubrious than usual.

'There must be a way,' said Mrs Pargeter. 'What's the date on the newspaper report?'

Truffler told her.

'Which would be just before the time that Normington Winthrop appeared in England. Having made his first fortune in Africa! Ooh, this is full of possibilities, Truffler!'

'I'll take your word for it,' he said, still sepulchrally low of voice.

'Can you email the cutting over to me?'

'Will do.'

'And meanwhile you'll see if you can find anything else relevant on the laptop or the papers you found at the house, won't you?'

'Of course I will, Mrs P.' He sounded offended that she felt she'd needed to ask the question.

There was no more thought of dozing now for Mrs Pargeter. She checked the laptop in the study to see if anything had come through yet from Truffler. No, so she went into the kitchen to put the kettle on for a cup of coffee. Then she forgot she'd done that and went to check the laptop once again. Nothing. Back to the kitchen to make the coffee. Forgetting to drink it, she returned to the study. And this time, yes, there was an email from Truffler.

Attached was the cutting from which he'd read to her. The copied paper looked yellowed and frail. Mrs Pargeter read through the whole of the report from which she'd just heard an extract. The rest of it added little to her stock of knowledge.

The only new information she received was the byline of the journalist who had written the piece. His name was Conrad Skeet.

And in her late husband's little black book there was someone who knew about journalists.

* * *

Ellie Fenchurch always acknowledged (to friends, not in the public press) the huge help Mr Pargeter had given her at the beginning of her career. He had met her when she tried to get an interview with him as part of a journalism course at a local polytechnic. He refused to do the interview, but was so impressed by her intelligence and tenacity that he paid for her to go on a better journalism course and started to use her skills to avoid unwelcome representation of his activities in the press.

Back then Ellie had been a gangly, long-limbed teenager. Now she was a tall woman in designer clothes whose weekly celebrity interview in one of the major Sunday newspapers brought her a huge and avid readership. Though she was renowned as Queen of the Hatchet Job, there still seemed to be an endless line of celebrities and politicians queuing up to have their reputations trashed by her.

Ellie Fenchurch recognized Mrs Pargeter's voice before she had time to identify herself. 'So good to hear from you,' she cooed in the voice whose Cockney origins she'd never contemplated hiding. 'Where're you living now?'

'Chigwell.'

'Oh, the house finally got built, did it? Congratulations. Do you know that means we're near neighbours?'

'Really?'

'Yes, I've still got my flat in the Barbican, but I like to get out of London every now and then – sign of age, probably – so I bought this house in a new development in Chigwell.'

'What an amazing coincidence.'

'Great coincidence. Come round and see it. Come and have a drink.'

'When?'

'Now. Give me your address and I'll send Gaston round to pick you up.'

Gaston turned out to be a young man of extraordinary beauty and very few words. Maybe he'd have had more words if Mrs Pargeter had spoken to him in French, but she'd never got very far with languages.

He appeared in a Porsche and drove Mrs Pargeter in under

five minutes to the home of his employer – or possibly lover; his lack of words led inevitably to a lack of such vital information.

The private gated development in which Ellie Fenchurch lived when she wasn't at the Barbican was brand-new. But whereas Mrs Pargeter's house had been constructed on Georgian principles, these dwellings were very clearly the products of 'modern architecture'. The roof looked as if it had been made from a single sheet of brushed silver, the supporting structure was all brushed silver pillars and everything else was glass. The whole development gave a new literalness to the expression 'living in a goldfish bowl', and the local window cleaners must have thought all their birthdays and Christmas had come at once.

But for Ellie herself the house was just as much a dream realized as the one Mrs Pargeter now inhabited would have been for her husband. Its minimalism – if that was the right word – fitted with the style she liked to project. This was also reflected in the clothes she wore – a silver top above black leggings and silver trainers. All hideously expensive designer kit which made her long thin body look wonderful.

As soon as she'd despatched Gaston to the fridge for some champagne, Ellie insisted on giving her guest the complete guided tour. As they moved from glass-walled room to glass-walled room and looked at carefully-placed artworks (most also made of glass), Mrs Pargeter found herself in danger of running out of her stock of appreciative platitudes. ('Oh, that is nice' – 'This is splendid' – 'Wonderful view from here' – 'Well, I never' and so on.)

Finally, they settled down in the first-floor sitting room with its perfect view of the other glass-fronted houses in the development. Gaston still did not speak as he poured champagne for them. Nor did he pour a glass for himself, suggesting perhaps that his role was that of a domestic servant. But the affectionate stroke Ellie gave to his hand when taking her glass from him suggested the possibility of another role. Equally, the speed with which he went downstairs, leaving the two woman in a tête-à-tête, made it perhaps more likely that he was a servant.

Mrs Pargeter did not let herself worry too much about this. Either she would have found out Gaston's role by the end of the evening, or she would not. How Ellie Fenchurch conducted her life was her own affair . . . though if she was having a sexual relationship with Gaston, she was very definitely moving into cougar territory.

And why not, thought Mrs Pargeter.

It had been a while since the two women had met, and Ellie was keen to fill her friend in with recent developments in her career. Mostly, these concerned celebrities interviewed and the attendant scurrilous gossip, which Mrs Pargeter enjoyed very much.

Who would have thought that a certain macho Hollywood action star always wore a lady's silk camisole next to his skin? Or that a former Home Secretary was addicted to a popular brand of cough syrup? Or, indeed, that a best-selling novelist had taken up tightrope-walking between skyscrapers simply because it was easier than writing? And that a well-known Cardinal had a tattoo of Marilyn Monroe on his lower back, so contrived that his two buttocks represented her breasts?

This was all such fun, so it was with reluctance that Mrs Pargeter finally dragged the conversation back to the purpose of her making contact. 'It's a long shot,' she said, 'but I'm trying to track down a journalist, and I was thinking – well, that's Ellie Fenchurch's world.'

'Certainly is. I reckon I know – or know about – everyone in the field. All the new kids on the block – and a lot of the tired old hacks.'

'I think the one I'm after would very definitely be in the second category by now.'

'So who is he?'

'Used to work on an expats' newspaper in the Congo some twenty years ago.'

Ellie Fenchurch let out a low whistle. 'You didn't tell me it was going to be *that* degree of difficulty. I reckon I know the personnel around Fleet Street pretty well – not, of course, that it is Fleet Street any more, but everyone still calls it that. My contacts in the Congo some twenty years ago are somewhat more limited.'

'Well, it would be wonderful if you could do a bit of detective work for me. And I think if you do manage to track him down, there could be rather a juicy scoop for you involved.'

Ellie Fenchurch's journalistic antennae were instantly alert. 'Give me the guy's name – that would be a start.'

'Conrad Skeet.'

Ellie looked at her in blank amazement. 'Well, this is your lucky day, Mrs P.'

'You mean you do know him?'

'Yes, I do. But I hate to think what the statistical chances of that happening—'

'Serendipity,' said Mrs Pargeter with an expression that was almost complacent. 'I've had a relatively bad run of luck recently – you know, on the investigation front. I deserve to have the dice falling my way for a change. So tell me about Conrad Skeet. Have you done one of your celebrity interviews with him?'

Ellie dismissed the idea with a puff of breath. 'No, no. He's far from a celebrity, but as a journalist he is interesting.'

'Why?'

'Because he does very little work – and seems to have done very little work for a long time – but he lives in a lifestyle that . . . well, a lifestyle that I certainly envy.'

'So what's the explanation for it?'

'I don't know. Which is why I find him intriguing.'

'Is it just a rich wife, Ellie? It often is.'

'Conrad's unmarried.'

'Family money?'

'I don't think so.'

'I mean, how well do you know him? Have you asked him where his money comes from?'

'No, but I know people who have.'

'And?'

'He clams up when he's asked about it. Very secretive.'

'Hm. And do you know where I might find him?'

'Yes. He's a near neighbour of mine at the Barbican. That's how we met. He owns a penthouse there.'

'Does he? Could you give me a number for him?'

Some instinct seemed to have told Gaston that their champagne glasses were empty, so he appeared to refill them. Ellie's touch on his arm this time showed that they were very definitely an item. But an item on her terms.

Good for you, Ellie, thought Mrs Pargeter.

TWENTY-FOUR

'I think the important thing about being a journalist is that one works by principle. Unless you're employed as a feature or leader writer, you're not there to push your opinions down your readers' throats. You are there to record what actually happens. And you do that with all the honesty of which you are capable. You don't kowtow to the prejudices of any editor or newspaper owner. You tell the truth. And that's the standard to which I have always aspired as a journalist. If I am not allowed to work on those terms, then I'd rather be out of work.'

As he uttered this fine speech, Conrad Skeet looked out over the unrivalled view of London commanded by his penthouse flat at the top of one of the three tall Barbican towers. It was one of the most sought-after addresses in the City of London, built on ground that had been devastated by Second World War bombing.

The journalist was probably pushing seventy and dressed in the smart blazer-and-cravat style of an earlier generation. He must have been a good-looking man earlier in his life, but was now rather fraying around the edges.

'And is that why,' asked Mrs Pargeter, 'you've done so relatively little work as a journalist over the years? Because you refused to do work that compromised your principles?'

'That is exactly what has happened, Mrs Pargeter. It's a pleasure to meet someone who has such an acute understanding of my position.'

Mrs Pargeter looked up from the cup of tea he had brought her and took in the contents of the room where they sat. There were paintings on the wall that had the air of being by people she should have heard of. The whole place breathed opulence.

'Mrs Pargeter,' said Conrad Skeet, and there was an edge of urgency in his voice. 'When you spoke to me on the phone, you said you were interested in the time when I was working in the Congo.'

'That's right.'

'And you want some information from me about that time?'

'Yes. That's what I'm after.'

'Might it possibly concern the man who became Sir Normington Winthrop?'

'I can return the compliment, Mr Skeet. You, too, have an acute understanding.'

'Thank you.' But there was still the urgency – or perhaps more than urgency, perhaps even fear – in his voice as he went on, 'I do know who you are, incidentally.'

'Who I am?' Mrs Pargeter feigned surprise. 'Oh, I'm nobody, really. Just a widow.'

'But I know who you are the widow *of.*'

'Oh?'

'I've done some research, Mrs Pargeter. I am a journalist, after all. And since you phoned me I have found out quite a lot about your late husband.'

'Really?'

'I know, for instance, the connection between him and the man called Anthony Hardcastle.'

'Oh? Did you meet Mr Hardcastle in the Congo?'

'I did. I also met Normington Winthrop.'

Mrs Pargeter tried desperately to hide her excitement. Finally, she was in the same room as someone who could tie the loose threads of the case together.

'As you know,' the journalist went on, 'Normington Winthrop – or Sir Normington Winthrop as he had by then become – died only a few weeks ago.'

'I did know that. I was at the funeral.'

'Ah. So was I. But there was no reason why we should meet there.'

'No.'

'Mrs Pargeter . . . not to put too fine a point on it . . . Sir Normington's death has put me in an unfortunate position.'

'Really?'

'Yes. The fact is . . . I was in the employ of Sir Normington Winthrop.'

'For your journalistic services?'

'You could say that.'

'For maintaining your journalistic principles?'

'You could say that too.'

Suddenly, Mrs Pargeter saw the whole picture. 'So what you're saying is that from the time of Anthony Hardcastle's death, Sir Normington has been paying you to keep quiet about what you know of the circumstances of that death?'

'Yes, that is what I am saying . . . though you do make it sound a bit mercenary.'

Well, what the hell is it if it's not mercenary? Mrs Pargeter did not give expression to this furious thought. Instead she said, 'But now he's dead, Mr Skeet, you find yourself without a paymaster?'

'Exactly.'

'So you're now looking for another paymaster?'

'Yes.'

'Or paymistress. Which is why you agreed to see me, why you rang me back after my initial call, once you had checked out my background . . . once you had ensured that I had enough money to keep you in the style to which over the years you have so easily become accustomed.'

'You have it in one, Mrs Pargeter.'

She opened her handbag. Inside, as well as Gizmo Gilbert's 'Zipper Zapper', which she had forgotten about, and other sorts of the usual feminine impedimenta, she had a cheque book. She knew that fewer and fewer people were using cheque books these days, but she found it very useful when paying small necessary sums to her husband's former associates (from real or invented bank accounts). Also, it was always very easy, if required, to stop a cheque.

She opened the book and flashed a pen at him. 'So how much are we talking?'

'In recent years, Sir Normington paid me ten thousand pounds a month.'

A hundred and twenty thou a year for keeping quiet about . . . what? Mrs Pargeter no longer had any doubt that Normington Winthrop had committed murder.

'Well,' she said, 'how about the same deal for you keeping quiet about it for me?'

She felt sure Conrad Skeet couldn't be following the logic through. If Sir Normington Winthrop was dead, then why would she possibly have a motive to keep his former crime covered up? But the glint of greed in the journalist's eye told her he wasn't thinking beyond the immediate cash.

'I'll pay you for three months,' Mrs Pargeter said airily as she wrote out a cheque for thirty thousand pounds. 'Then I'll set up a regular direct debit.' She handed the cheque across. 'So now, Mr Skeet, I think you'd better tell me what happened in the Congo all those years ago.'

He took the cheque, folded it and placed it in the inside pocket of his blazer. Then, with considerable pride in his voice, he began his narrative.

'It was a pretty rough place back then. Still is from all accounts. But twenty years ago there were all kinds of local disputes – some going back to ancient tribal conflicts, some about mineral rights, some just because people liked the idea of blowing other people's heads off. But to do that, of course, they needed weapons. And though a lot of the grunt work was done by locals, the bosses of the gun-running businesses were mostly white – from South Africa, from the States, from England, from everywhere.

'Normington Winthrop was one of the top dogs in that field. He was from South Africa originally – Jo'burg, I think – but he set up base in Kindu and pretty soon controlled all the weapons supply around there. The locals respected him. He was a fair man – well, as fair as anyone could be in that kind of business – and when he made a deal he stuck to the terms they agreed.

'And his deals were never in cash, always in gold. There was plenty of unofficial or illegal mining going on round there, so it was like a handy currency. Normington doesn't trust the local banks – which is a very shrewd calculation, as they're all corrupt as hell – so he keeps his gold in a chest in his home, which is guarded twenty-four/seven. He does a lot of his deals at the house, and when he doesn't he takes the gold with him in a leather knapsack.

'So he was kind of set up for life. He had his delivery lines in place for sourcing the weapons, he knew which local officials might need their palms greased and he ran a very tight ship. He was married, too, to a local woman. All was fine until suddenly this guy Tony Hardcastle turns up.'

'I believe,' said Mrs Pargeter, 'when he worked with my husband he was called Hair-Trigger Hardcastle.'

'Called that out in the Congo too. Anyway, this Hardcastle character is very determined to challenge Normington Winthrop's monopoly on the local gun-running scene, but he plays it quite cool. Makes it seem like he's suggesting them pooling their resources. He has access to some supplies of weapons that Normington doesn't, so it looks like he really is bringing something to the table. And they form a kind of uneasy partnership. Neither really trusts the other, but they jog along and, using both their sources of weapons, the business does become more profitable.

'Then, suddenly, they disappear. First sign something's wrong is there's a raid on Normington Winthrop's house in Kindu. Guards all shot dead, and – no great surprise – the chest of gold isn't there any more. Nor's his wife. God knows what happened to her. And Winthrop and Hardcastle also seem to have vanished off the face of the earth. Then, a few months later, the body of a white man is found in the jungle.'

'As reported by you in that press cutting I saw,' said Mrs Pargeter.

'Exactly.'

'Hair-Trigger Hardcastle shot dead,' she went on, 'with the implication that Normington Winthrop topped him. And within a year of that Winthrop's appeared in London, where he starts to build a legitimate career.'

Conrad Skeet nodded in admiration. 'You have done your homework, Mrs Pargeter. And, of course, the word you've just used – "legitimate" – is a relative term. At the beginning of his career in England, Normington Winthrop is still using the contacts he had built up while he was involved in illegal gun-running. But he's not selling the goods to local guerrillas any more. Gradually, he gets himself closer and closer to government contacts. In a relatively short time he's acting as a salesman for the United Kingdom's arms trade.'

'And he funded the start of his legitimate career with the gold that he'd accumulated in the Congo?'

'Yes, he must have smuggled it out of the country somehow – not a difficult task for someone with the contacts he had.'

Mrs Pargeter nodded as she pieced things together. 'Then he starts to worm his way up into London society. He meets Lady Helena Whatever-her-maiden-name-was, and marrying her gets him even further away from his criminal roots.'

'That's how it worked, yes.'

'Then you came to London, Mr Skeet, and heard about the highly successful businessman Sir Normington Winthrop – assuming he was knighted by then?'

'He was.'

'And you realized that what you knew about his past could actually be a rather valuable commodity?'

'That's a very good way of putting it, Mrs Pargeter. So I contacted him.'

'Didn't you think you were taking a risk? After all, he'd shot Hair-Trigger Hardcastle and presumably the guards at his house. Hair-Trigger's wife as well, perhaps?'

'Yes, but that was all in the Congo. Murders tend to be more closely investigated in London than they are out there. Paying me off was much less of a risk than killing me would have been. And, though very welcome to yours truly, for him the money was just a fleabite.'

'And now he's dead, the payments have come to an end?'

'Yes. Well, his accounts were all frozen when he died, but I have made contact with his widow.'

'Helena.'

'Exactly. I had to be a little circumspect in how I described the services for which Sir Normington had paid me. I said I was an "Image Consultant" and it was my task to ensure that press coverage of her husband was always friendly. And I asked whether she would be continuing with the monthly retainer which her husband had agreed to pay me.'

Mrs Pargeter chuckled. 'And she told you to get lost.'

Conrad Skeet looked offended by this, but admitted that, though she hadn't used those exact words, that had been the gist of Lady Winthrop's response. Then he gestured to the cheque on the table. 'Which is why I am so grateful to have found another generous paymistress.'

Mrs Pargeter nodded and smiled. But her mind was racing. She had a lot to do. First she had to get on to her bank and stop the cheque. Then she'd contact Truffler and Erin, tell them the new information and get them to find out as much corroborating detail as possible. They'd compile a dossier, which would be passed over to Ellie Fenchurch. Though her main job was doing the Sunday interview, she still had a good relationship with the editorial staff on her paper's weekly version. There was nothing they would like better than a massive exposé under her byline of the criminal past of the late Sir Normington Winthrop.

'Well, thank you so much for your time, Mr Skeet,' said Mrs Pargeter, gathering up her handbag.

'My pleasure. And I have been handsomely paid for it. So handsomely that I think I must let you know the pay-off to the narrative.'

'One pay-off for another pay-off?'

'Beautifully put.' He got himself back into storytelling mode. 'A few months after the discovery of the body in the jungle, I was in Jo-burg for a bit of R and R. One morning I was sitting in the sun outside a bar with a nice Castle Lager, when I saw someone I recognized walking past. I put down some money for the beer and followed him at a distance. He hadn't seen me, so I was quite safe.

'I guess I thought he was probably there doing something with the gold – banking it, exchanging it, because Jo-burg's such a centre for that trade. But, no, he didn't go into any of the many banks there were along that stretch of road. He went into a very modern looking office. Once he was out of sight I checked the brass plate on the door. It was a consultancy in plastic surgery.'

'So Normington Winthrop was taking another step in erasing his past?'

'Yes. Except that the person I followed wasn't Normington Winthrop.'

'Oh?'

'It was Hair-Trigger Hardcastle.'

TWENTY-FIVE

G ary's Bentley was parked on a double yellow line outside the entrance to the Barbican Theatre. 'Where to?' he asked.

Her mind was so full of new thoughts that she had to untangle them before she could come up with an answer. 'I need to see Truffler, so his office.'

'I was just in touch with him, Mrs P, and he's still working with Erin at her place.'

'Then Erin's place it is.'

As they drove north and watched the office blocks and City institutions give way to residential housing, Mrs Pargeter said little. She just tried to think of all the possible ramifications of her new stock of knowledge. The only time she spoke was when she phoned her bank to cancel the thirty-thousand-pound cheque she'd just given to Conrad Skeet.

Erin's house looked exactly as it had the last time Mrs Pargeter had seen it. Front room minimalist, back room full of neatly shelved old files. The fact that the entire contents had been removed and replaced by Kelvin Mitchell had left no trace.

Once they were all supplied with coffee, Mrs Pargeter said, 'Now, I really have got some news.'

'So have I,' said Truffler.

'I cannot believe,' she said, 'that yours is quite as sensational as mine, so do you mind if I go first?'

'Of course not.'

'Go for it,' said Gary.

Mrs Pargeter looked at him fondly. 'Sorry, I could have told you this in the car, but I didn't want to go through the whole lot twice.'

'Fully understood.' He grinned back at her. 'Fire away.'

And Mrs Pargeter told them everything that she had learned

from Conrad Skeet. At the end there was a long silence. They were all too surprised and impressed to speak.

Finally, Truffler said, 'So it never was Normington Winthrop who came to London. It was Hair-Trigger Hardcastle all the time.'

'Hair-Trigger Hardcastle with a bit of cosmetic surgery, yes.'

'Which makes Sir Normington Winthrop's background even dodgier,' Erin observed. 'A multiple murderer, who spent all his life in England under a false identity.'

'And him such a pillar of the establishment,' said Gary. 'Makes you wonder about the rest of the Great and the Good, doesn't it?'

'Well, I've always had my doubts about the lot of them,' said Truffler.

'Anyway, Mrs Pargeter, what are you planning to do with all this information?' asked Erin.

'What I'd like to do is for you and Truffler to build it all up into a dossier.'

'No problem. What, and then we pass it over to the police?'

Mrs Pargeter's face wrinkled in disagreement. 'I don't think that's really appropriate in this case.'

'Then what do you want to do with it?'

'Pass it over to Ellie Fenchurch.'

'The journalist?'

'Exactly. Then she can get a front page exposé that'll really shake things up.'

'Great idea,' said Truffler. 'She can—'

Mrs Pargeter raised a hand to stop him. 'There is, however, one person whose permission we must get first.' She took out her mobile and called up a number from the memory.

To her surprise, a man's voice answered. 'Lady Winthrop's phone,' it said.

The penny dropped for Mrs Pargeter. Of course – Sir Normington's widow was still under protection. 'Napper,' she said, 'it's Mrs Pargeter. Could I have a word with Helena?'

'Of course.'

Mrs Pargeter gave an edited version of what she had found out about Lady Winthrop's late husband, and then said, 'I want to break this to the press. Do you mind?'

Helena Winthrop's cut-glass voice was dipped in venom as she replied, 'Mind? Why'd I mind? Publish whatever you want. It will be a welcome revenge for me after all I had to put up with from the bastard!'

Something seemed to have put some fire into the painfully correct Lady Winthrop. And Mrs Pargeter had a strong feeling that that something could have been Napper Johnson.

The excitements of Mrs Pargeter's revelations had driven all other thoughts from the brains assembled in Erin Jarvis's office, and Truffler Mason had to remind them that he also had some news on the case. 'It's not as dramatic as yours, Mrs P, but it does make a lot of things fall into place.'

'What is it?'

Truffler gestured towards Erin's laptop and asked, 'May I?'

'Of course.'

He pressed various keys and scrolled through a few screens before he found what he was looking for. It was a scanned black and white photograph of what he identified as the third annual conference of BROG. 'The "Britons, Restore Our Greatness" party,' he glossed for those who might not know the acronym.

At the front of the picture was a rather younger Derek Bardon, spouting at a microphone. Seated behind him was a row of glowering men. Amongst them, though he was wearing long hair and a youthful beard, it was quite easy to identify Edmund Grainger.

'Well, that kind of figures,' said Mrs Pargeter.

TWENTY-SIX

Mrs Pargeter didn't like waiting, and she had rather a lot of it to do in the next few days. It took a while for Truffler and Erin to check and verify all the information that was to be included in their dossier. And once it had been passed over to Ellie Fenchurch, more checking and verification were required before her bosses felt that it was safe to publish.

As soon as she had done a draft of her exposé, Ellie sent a copy to Mrs Pargeter, who thought it was brilliant. 'If I were your editor, I'd run it tomorrow,' she said on the phone.

'Yes, but they have to be very careful from the legal point of view. This is explosive stuff. If there are any inaccuracies in it, we could be in big trouble.'

'What, you mean libel? I didn't think you could libel someone who's dead. And Sir Normington Winthrop is very definitely dead.'

'Yes, but there are other names in there – names of people who're still alive.'

Mrs Pargeter wasn't sufficiently familiar with the law to be able to argue further. Her late husband had frequently said, 'Melita, my love, you only need to know enough about the law to keep on the right side of it,' and as in all things she had followed his principle.

She tried to fill the time by helping Sammy Pinkerton with her wedding plans, but her mind wasn't really on them. Fortunately, Sammy was in too ecstatic a mood to notice any lack of concentration from her benefactress. She and her Kelvin were more of an item than ever, and she was totally unfazed by the prospect of becoming Mrs Mitchell rather than Mrs Stockett.

She was also very relieved to know that her fiancé had given up his life of crime. Kelvin, now seeing his father as a very different kind of role model, had immediately started investigating how to join the police force, a career choice with which Sammy was much happier. He even contacted some cousins on his mother's side of the family who, following the example of her Chief Constable father, had joined the Met. Once Kelvin Mitchell got an idea fixed in his mind, nothing could shake it out.

Sammy's only gripe was that she seemed to see her fiancé even less than usual over the next few days. Whatever he was doing took him away from the flat at least as much as his burglary site-casing had. And he was equally unhelpful when she asked him what he was doing. 'It's a secret mission,' was all he would say. 'An investigation of my own. If it's brought to a successful conclusion, I think it could be a very good calling card for me to take to the Met.'

For Mrs Pargeter the days passed slowly, and she began to wonder whether Ellie's bosses were ever going to give the go-ahead for her scoop. She pottered round the Chigwell house, unable to concentrate on anything for long. She even occasionally switched on daytime television, only to discover how devastatingly accurate Holy Smirke's assessment of it had been. She twitched around the house in a way that did not accord with her usual eternally positive manner.

Finally, on the Saturday morning she had a call from Ellie Fenchurch.

'It's been green-lighted,' the journalist said, with a sigh of relief.

'They're going to run it?'

'Sure. Tomorrow. They say it's the kind of story that needs the space only a Sunday paper can give it.'

'And they haven't made you cut anything out?'

'No, it'll be printed in exactly the version that you've read.'

'Wonderful.'

'Yes. I'm very pleased with it. Also . . .' said Ellie without false modesty, 'something with my byline on it sells papers. And for me it's been great, going back to my roots as an investigative journalist, before I got involved in all this celebrity interview nonsense.'

It was on the front page of the paper that fell on Mrs Pargeter's doormat that Sunday morning. There was a colour photograph of Sir Normington Winthrop with Derek Bardon, both black-tied at some fund-raising dinner.

The headline read: 'CRIMINAL PAST OF BROG FUNDRAISER.'

Mrs Pargeter went out to one of her favourite local restaurants for a full Sunday roast with all the trimmings. To celebrate, she had a whole bottle of champagne to herself.

When she got back to the house she indulged in a very comfortable doze on her sitting room sofa, once again ensuring that when she returned to consciousness Gary's cat would be out of her eyeline.

She was woken by a call from a very ecstatic Ellie Fenchurch. 'The story's really gone down big. You should see all the stuff about it on Facebook and Twitter.'

'I'm afraid I don't do either of those,' said Mrs Pargeter a little primly.

'Well, you'd better watch the evening news. It's going to be *the* big story then.'

It was the lead item on the early evening news. There had been no reaction yet from Derek Bardon at his party headquarters, but a political correspondent couldn't see how much longer the leader could continue in his job. BROG was finished. And though the correspondent's stance of impartiality did not allow him to say it, his tone implied, 'And good riddance!'

Mrs Pargeter also watched the late evening news to see if there had been any developments. There had. Derek Bardon did not wish to be interviewed, but a still photograph of him filled the screen. He had issued a statement, saying that he was 'shocked and disappointed' by the revelations in a Sunday newspaper and that he 'would be consulting his lawyers and considering his position'.

But it was the second item on the bulletin that really shook up Mrs Pargeter. A journalist called Conrad Skeet had been found shot dead in his Barbican flat.

TWENTY-SEVEN

The phone rang before the television news had finished. It was Truffler. A very urgent-sounding Truffler. 'You're in danger, Mrs P! But don't worry, we're on our way. Gary and I will be with you as soon as we can. Lock all the doors, and don't let anyone in!'

'But who am I in danger from?'

'Whoever killed Skeet. Which could well be Edmund Grainger. And if it's someone else, they can easily find Skeet's connection to Ellie's exposé, which means they can find you too. I don't think they're trying to silence people any longer. Now it's just revenge – payback time.'

'But isn't Ellie in danger too?'

'Probably. I managed to prise Napper away from Helena Winthrop and sent him and some of his crew to protect Ellie.'

'Good.'

'See you very shortly, Mrs P.'

It was dark outside, and she didn't know where she would feel safest. Her kitchen was the cosiest room in the house, but it was too near the great expanse of darkness that was her back garden. No, she was probably better off in the sitting room.

She contemplated switching the television on. Not because there was anything she wanted to watch, but it might give her the illusion of doing something. Second thoughts stopped her, however. The noise from the television might drown out the sounds of someone trying to break in to the house.

She couldn't help feeling nervous. She crossed to the mantelpiece and looked at the unsmiling photograph of the late Mr Pargeter. 'You got out of worse scrapes than this one, love. And I'll get out of it too.' But the level of confidence in her words was not reflected in her mind.

She found she was looking at Gary's wretched cat, so turned away.

She sat down on the sofa and took the little black book out of her handbag. Flicking idly through it, she didn't know what she was looking for. It was just a link to her late husband that gave her strength in moments of crisis.

Unwittingly, she found the section entitled 'Armourers'. And she scrutinized the name of 'Normington Winthrop', the trigger of her whole investigation. If she hadn't found that in the little black book, she would never have gone to the funeral, never have become involved in the strange sequence of events that had ensued.

And as she looked at the name, the explanation came to her. She remembered Truffler Mason commenting on the roughness of the surface of the paper on which it had been written and the way the ink had run. Instantly, she realised that it wasn't just that the entry had been made a long time ago and the paper had suffered over the years. The truth was much simpler than that.

The first entry in the 'Armourers' category had been 'Tony Hardcastle'. It had to be. He was one of the original three, the founding core of the operation. Mrs Pargeter's late husband, Gizmo Gilbert and Tony Hardcastle.

And when Hair-Trigger had cheated Mr Pargeter and stopped working with him, her husband had expunged all record of him from the little black book. Erased the entry with one of those hard ink-rubbers which always left the paper rough (and frequently broke through it). Then, when the man called Normington Winthrop had come to England, in spite of his plastic surgery Mr Pargeter had recognized him as his former collaborator, Hair-Trigger Hardcastle. So he'd written the new name in the space where the old one had been.

Now Mrs Pargeter looked closely at the smudged entry she could see that the ink was less faded than on some of the subsequent names. Which only went to confirm her developing outline of what had happened.

Then, logical in all things, her late husband had re-entered the name of Tony Hardcastle further down the list of 'Armourers' and put a line through it. Because, whichever way you looked at it, the old Tony Hardcastle was dead.

So her husband had known all about the real identity of

Normington Winthrop. Mrs Pargeter felt pretty sure, though, that he hadn't known about the murderous methods by which Hair-Trigger Hardcastle had achieved the transformation. If he'd been aware of that, Mr Pargeter, who had always had a great respect for justice, would surely have done something about it.

In a strange way, having interpreted the processes of his mind made her for a moment feel very close to her absent spouse. Also feeling great glee at having worked out the explanation of those distant events, Mrs Pargeter looked up from the little black book.

And it was when she did that that she saw a tall, broad-shouldered man outlined in the doorway to the kitchen.

Edmund Grainger. And he had a very purposeful-looking automatic pistol in his hand.

'Mrs Pargeter,' he said in a voice bleached of emotion, 'I knew when I first met you at the funeral that you'd be trouble.'

For some insane reason she thought that a cheeky response might be the best one. 'Glad to be of service.'

His rigid expression did not change. 'You probably don't realize the extent of the damage you've done.'

'The aim was for it to be as extensive as possible,' she explained in a friendly manner.

'You've ruined BROG. You've ruined everything I've been working to build up over many years.'

'Well, I don't think I'm going to my grave worrying too much about that,' said Mrs Pargeter with an assumed breeziness. Too late, she rather regretted her words. The mention of 'going to her grave' might put ideas in Edmund Grainger's head. Though she was rather afraid the ideas were already there.

Get him talking, she told herself. Get him on to a subject he really cares about. She could only think of one. 'Were you involved with BROG right from the beginning?' she asked.

And, sure enough, he couldn't stop himself from replying. 'Yes, I was. I met Derek Bardon at a Conservative Party Conference years ago. Back then we both hoped that the Tories might have the solutions to the country's problems, but we pretty soon realized that, like the rest of the existing parties, they were full of nothing but wind and broken promises. We went off to a pub to have a few disillusioned drinks. And it was then Derek told me about his plans for a completely new political party – one that would blow away all the cobwebs from the corridors of power, one that would make the British once again feel proud to be British.'

'So it started with just the two of you?'

'Yes, but we very soon found that there were millions of people in this country who were experiencing just the same kind of frustration with recent governments as we were.'

Mrs Pargeter dared to be combative. 'Well, it seems you somehow failed to get all those millions to come out and vote for you, didn't you?'

The combative approach proved not to be a good one. 'Shut up, Mrs Pargeter!' roared Edmund Grainger on a burst of dangerous anger. 'You know nothing about politics, do you?'

'I must admit that there are other subjects in life that I've generally found more interesting. And I do feel terribly sorry for those poor MPs who spend their lives going from one boring meeting to another and are not allowed to express their own opinions but have to follow a party line in spite of—'

He overrode her. 'Well, if you knew anything about the subject, you would also know that nothing comes for nothing. Every political party needs funding.'

'Which is where Sir Normington Winthrop becomes part of the equation, is it?'

'Yes.'

'Where did you meet him?'

'At a Labour Party Conference the year after Derek and I had come up with the idea for BROG.'

'And he had the same kind of ideas as you had?'

'Yes,' said Edmund Grainger fervently. 'Norm shared exactly the same kind of disillusionment as we did with the current state of politics. As we discovered at the conference, what Labour were offering was just as useless as the Tories' solutions. They were all talking tired, old-fashioned politics.'

'But surely,' Mrs Pargeter suggested politely, 'BROG was talking even more old-fashioned politics? I mean, going back to the days of the British Empire, sending immigrants home to—'

'Mrs Pargeter, just shut up about things you don't understand!'

'Sorry,' she said, duly chastised. 'But Sir Normington offered to fund BROG, did he?'

'Yes. He'd just come back from the Congo, and he'd witnessed first-hand the terrible effects that the wrong kind of British colonial policy had had there, and—'

'Erm, sorry to interrupt you,' said Mrs Pargeter.

'What?'

'But I think you'll find that the Congo was not colonized by the British. It was colonized by the Belgians, so if there's anyone you want to accuse of the wrong kind of colonial policy you should—'

'Will you just shut up! I've come here to kill you, not to listen to your half-baked ideas about international history.'

'Well, I just thought that if you and Derek Bardon and Sir Normington Winthrop were setting up a party trying to correct the failures of British colonial policy based on the model of a country where Belgian colonial policy was—'

'Shut it!' he shouted, so loudly that she did.

With a meek change of direction, she said, 'So, as soon as he heard about the party, Sir Normington agreed to fund BROG?'

'Yes,' Grainger conceded.

'And at that time did you know about his past in Africa?'

'We knew he'd just come back from there, obviously.'

'But did you know what he'd done there?'

'He'd made a huge fortune in the munitions business.'

'Gun-running.'

'It doesn't matter what you call it. When Norm arrived in England, the slate of his past was wiped clean.'

'Oh, was it? So you didn't know what he'd done out in the Congo?'

'It didn't matter. He offered a lifeline to BROG. A lifeline Derek and I were very happy to grasp with both hands.'

'So neither you nor Derek knew exactly where his money had come from?'

'Of course we did. I told you. The munitions business.'

'Hm.' Mrs Pargeter paused for a moment. 'But you can see that it'd make a difference – to the image of BROG – if you knew that the so-called Sir Normington Winthrop's fortune had been amassed by Hair-Trigger Hardcastle committing multiple murders and then assuming a new identity?'

'I don't know what you're talking about.'

But the way Grainger looked down when he said the words told Mrs Pargeter that he was lying. She pressed home her small advantage. 'So you knew from the start the illicit source of Sir Normington's fortune? You knew he was really Hair-Trigger Hardcastle? No wonder he was prepared to pay for Conrad Skeet's silence.'

An unpleasant grin spread across Edmund Grainger's face. 'We don't have to worry about Conrad Skeet any more.' It was tantamount to a confession of murder. 'And pretty soon –' he looked along the barrel of his gun – 'we won't have to worry about you either, Mrs Pargeter.'

Keep them talking, keep them talking. She remembered that advice from countless thrillers and B-movies. When confronted by a man with a gun keen to shoot you, a life-saving tactic is to engage them in light conversation for as long as possible. And she hadn't done too badly already on keeping him talking. Could she manage to do so for a bit longer?

'Well,' she began, 'there is an issue of principle at stake here, and—'

But Edmund Grainger had clearly read the same thrillers and watched the same B-movies. He knew how inadvisable it was for people bent on murder to allow themselves to become engaged in conversation. He also realized that he had broken that golden rule, and Mrs Pargeter had already engaged him in far more conversation than was appropriate in such circumstances.

'Don't bother talking,' he said, rather belatedly. 'It won't save you. I've come here with the simple purpose of killing you, and that is exactly what I am going to do.'

He moved a little nearer her and raised the gun to point directly at the middle of her forehead.

Oh dear, thought Mrs Pargeter, this really is it. She wondered what she could do. Phoning the police never occurred to her. But getting in touch with *SomeoneAtTheOtherEndOfTheLine.com* . . . that was a thought. Trouble was, there was no time for anything like that.

Shortly, she told herself desperately, I will find out if there is an afterlife where I will be reunited with my husband. But she still thought the chances were against it. Just as the chances were against her surviving the next fifteen seconds.

There was a sudden commotion behind Edmund Grainger. He half-turned as a figure in black jeans and hoodie, face hidden by a black scarf, launched itself at him.

The newcomer had the advantage of surprise, and he wrapped Grainger's body in a bear hug, immobilizing his arms by his sides. The gun went off, making, Mrs Pargeter noticed, a rather unsightly dent in her woodblock flooring.

Edmund Grainger was very strong, but his captor appeared to be stronger. Still controlling the man's body in his hugging grip, he manoeuvred the resisting criminal in the direction of the fireplace. Then, using his own head for extra power, he smashed Grainger's forehead against the jutting marble shelf. The second time he did it, the pistol slipped from the potential murderer's hand and his body slithered down to the floor.

The man in black kicked the gun across the floor towards Mrs Pargeter, who picked it up. Then he whipped out a pair of handcuffs, brought the bleary Edmund Grainger's hands round behind his back and snapped the cuffs on his wrist.

His victim was by now conscious and trying to stand up. The captor placed a hand on his shoulder and announced, 'This is a citizen's arrest. Edmund Grainger, you are under arrest for threatening to kill Mrs Pargeter.' He produced a mobile phone. 'A video of which action I fortunately managed to capture on this. And I'm sure when the police interview you, they will find a whole list of other crimes with which to charge you.'

Edmund Grainger was still too fuddled to make any reply.

The man in black whipped the scarf off his face and pulled his hood down to reveal the ash blond hair of Kelvin Mitchell.

'I've been following him for days, Mrs Pargeter,' he said. 'Couldn't follow him into the Barbican, but I've got video of him entering and exiting the building this afternoon. I think that'll put him firmly in the frame for the murder of Conrad Skeet.'

'Well, Kelvin,' said Mrs Pargeter, 'I can't thank you enough. I know the expression "you saved my life" is bandied about far too much, but in this case you actually did.'

'No worries. I was glad to do it,' said Kelvin Mitchell, longing for the day when he would not be making citizen's arrests but proper police ones.

TWENTY-EIGHT

At that moment they heard the screeching of a Ferrari coming to a halt on gravel. As ever, Gary had selected the right car for the job and the drive out to Chigwell had been a testament to the skills he'd developed back when he was a getaway driver.

He and Truffler were considerably relieved to find that no harm had come to Mrs Pargeter and full of admiration for the way Kelvin Mitchell had captured Edmund Grainger.

He glowed in their commendation. 'Used a bit of my old skills too,' he said. 'Your security system's good, Mrs Pargeter, but not good enough, I'm afraid. I had no problem entering the property.'

'I'll get it seen to,' she said.

'But the question is – what are we going to do about him?' asked Truffler, pointing towards the handcuffed man sitting on the floor.

'I've worked that out,' Kelvin replied. 'I'm going to drive him in my van to the headquarters of the City of London Police station in Wood Street and turn him in.'

'That's very brave of you,' said Mrs Pargeter, mindful of her late husband's dictum that one should never have more to do with the police than was absolutely necessary.

'There's no danger of the cops letting him go?' asked Truffler uneasily.

'No way. Not when I've shown them my video evidence.'

'Well, in that case,' said Mrs Pargeter, 'I think it's a very good idea.' She looked down at her unwelcome guest. 'The sooner he's out of my house, the happier I will be.'

Truffler and Gary manhandled Edmund Grainger out to Kelvin's van, and it was a moment before Mrs Pargeter noticed that the young man hadn't gone with them. Instead, he stood behind a sofa, twisting the black scarf rather nervously in his hands.

'I'm sorry, is there a problem, Kelvin?' she asked.

'Well, it is rather awkward . . .' he began tentatively.

'I'm sure it's nothing that can't be easily sorted out,' she reassured him. 'Is it something with you and Sammy? Because I'd have done anything for the two of you even before you saved my life, but now—'

'No, it's nothing to do with me and Sammy. Everything's fine with me and Sammy.'

'Good.' She waited for him to fill the silence, but he didn't, just continued to stand there winding the scarf around his hands. 'What is it, Kelvin?'

He shook back his blond fringe with an attempt at assertiveness. 'The fact is, Mrs Pargeter, that I have really enjoyed the contact I've had with you over the last few weeks.'

'It's mutual. Been a pleasure to get to know you too, Kelvin.'

'And I can't thank you enough for your generosity to Sammy and me over the wedding arrangements, and—'

'I've been delighted to help out. My husband, I'm sure, would have felt the same. We owed something to Sammy's father, and we're making it up to his daughter.'

'Yes, well, that brings me to the point of what I'm saying. You know what Sammy's father did for a living, don't you?'

Mrs Pargeter smiled ingenuously. 'Graphic artist, wasn't he?'

'The fact is, Mrs Pargeter, that Sammy's father was a forger and a crook!'

'Oh, I didn't know that,' she said mildly.

'Well, it's true. And all the people we've been working with . . .' He gestured towards the front garden. 'Truffler and Gary, Napper . . . they're all crooks.'

'I think you should be wary of making such allegations,' said Mrs Pargeter with some asperity. 'Truffler Mason runs a legitimate detective agency, Gary has a very successful legitimate car-hire business, and Napper Johnson runs one of the country's foremost legitimate public relations companies. And the detail they have in common is that all of them were helped when they were setting up their businesses by my late husband. Who was a very good judge of the character and honesty of an individual.'

'Yes, but the fact is, Mrs Pargeter, that your late husband was a . . .' Kelvin's words trickled to a halt.

'Was a what?' she prompted. But still the words didn't come. 'Hmm?'

The boy started off on another tack. 'Listen, Mrs Pargeter, you know that I am planning to join the police force?'

'Yes. Following in the footsteps of your late father.'

'Exactly. And the point is that once I am established in my future career, though I will undoubtedly have contact with criminals in the line of duty . . .'

'Undoubtedly.'

'I will not be able to fraternize with them.'

'Sorry, Kelvin. What exactly are you saying?'

'I am saying that when I am a member of the police force I will not be able to be friends with people who have criminal connections!' He looked relieved at having got that off his chest.

'And is that all you were going to say?' asked Mrs Pargeter.

'Yes, it is.'

'Oh, I'm so relieved. The build-up you gave it, I thought it was going to be something much worse.'

'What d'you mean?'

'All I mean is that it's a relief to know that you and I think so alike about things.'

'Sorry?'

'Well, I couldn't agree with you more, Kelvin.'

'Mm?'

'I've never been able to be friends with people who have criminal connections,' said Mrs Pargeter with a huge smile. 'And I look forward to seeing lots more of you and Sammy in the future, Kelvin.'

The boy went out to drive Edmund Grainger to the police station. Truffler and Gary returned to the sitting room. Mrs Pargeter offered them a drink to celebrate the successful outcome of the case, but they both demurred, Gary because he was driving and Truffler because he had an early start in the morning. 'Got to get back to the day-to-day business of tracing flighty wives and errant husbands,' he said mournfully.

Mrs Pargeter didn't mind their going. She was feeling quite weary after the tensions of the day and thought going to bed straight away was her best option.

But she did just casually switch the television back on and found a news channel where a front man and two pundits were talking about the political implications of the exposure of BROG. Which she did find rather interesting, and she had soon been sitting there for more than half an hour.

'Of course,' said the front man as a huge picture of Derek Bardon filled the screen behind him, 'we're still waiting for a more detailed statement from the leader of BROG, but he seems to have vanished off the face of the earth.'

'Oh, I wouldn't say that,' said a voice behind Mrs Pargeter.

TWENTY-NINE

' I 've been here for a while,' said Derek Bardon almost languidly. 'I got in at the same time as Edmund, fortunately unnoticed by your superhero in black. And then I found a very convenient broom cupboard in your kitchen, where I have been ever since, listening to everything that's gone on here.'

'What do you want with me?'

'Revenge.'

'For what?'

'For ruining my entire life. My dreams of political power have been dealt a death-blow. And that's all down to you, Mrs Pargeter. It's all your fault. Why did you do it?'

'I think the crimes of Sir Normington Winthrop should be a matter of public knowledge. Though it's not always the case, in this one I think the truth had to come out. It's a matter of principle with me.'

'Very admirable, I'm sure, Mrs Pargeter. But principles are not going to save your life.' His face reddened as a burst of anger swept through him. 'If you only knew the damage you have caused! Not just to me but to this country.'

'How've I done that?'

'By killing BROG as a political force. We were starting to make serious inroads into the seat of political power. Getting more and more local councillors. Only a matter of time before we get an MEP, then someone at the Westminster Parliament. It's a matter of time and momentum, which was building very nicely. And you have destroyed all that.'

'Sorry,' said Mrs Pargeter, though she didn't feel very sorry.

'And without BROG there as a moderating force, this whole country will go to hell in a handcart.'

Mrs Pargeter, who had never before heard BROG described as 'a moderating force', listened as he went on, getting ever more vehement.

'There'll be unrestricted immigration, good British jobs

taken by foreigners. And that'll only be the start of it. Under the current government – or the other lot; they're both equally useless – there doesn't seem to be any concept of the threat the country is under. Already there are Muslims on every street, in every town council. It's only a matter of time before this whole country's run by them!'

'And BROG could have put a stop to that?'

'Of course it could. We are the only British party whose manifesto promises a policy of *sending all immigrants back where they belong*! And there are an enormous number of people in this country who support that policy.'

'Well, I don't know many people who support it.'

'All that means is that you mix with the wrong sort of people. Woolly-minded liberals. Not the real people of Britain – the ones who are proud of our island heritage and who want to keep foreigners out, just as the pilots of the Battle of Britain kept the hated Germans at bay.'

'If I've ruined the chances of people who think like that getting into power,' said Mrs Pargeter, 'then I think I've done rather a good job.'

'No, you haven't! You've destroyed everything! And that is why I'm going to kill you.' As he spoke, he drew from his pocket an automatic pistol identical to the one with which Edmund Grainger had threatened Mrs Pargeter only a few hours earlier.

'If you shoot me,' she said, trying to sound cool, 'you won't get away with it. You'll be found out and spend the rest of your life in jail.'

'I don't care about that. I don't care about anything. My career's ruined. Everything I've worked for has been smashed to pieces. And the only thing that's going to make me feel mildly better is to put a bullet through your head!'

The look in Derek Bardon's eyes now was truly scary. Mrs Pargeter realized how loose his grip on reality was and what real danger she was in. She clutched her handbag to her, rose from the sofa and moved towards the mantelpiece, which was spattered with a few spots of blood from Edmund Grainger's forehead.

But Derek Bardon moved straight after her, raising the

gun in just the same way her previous would-be assassin had done.

Then, she'd been saved by Kelvin Mitchell. But he was far off, handing Edmund Grainger over to the City of London police. Truffler and Gary too were by now a good half hour away. They couldn't return to save her in the few seconds of life she had remaining.

If she was going to get out of her current predicament, she was going to have to do it on her own initiative.

Suddenly, a thought came to her. Reaching deftly inside her handbag she felt the reassuring outline of Gizmo Gilbert's prototype 'Zipper Zapper'. Keeping it still hidden, she pointed it towards her attacker's groin and pressed the control.

Now, men are funny – almost obsessed – about their zips. They all live in terror of being seen in public with their zips undone. It is for them a deep humiliation, inadequately understood by the other gender.

So, as Derek Bardon felt the tug of his zip descending, he could not help himself from looking downwards.

And in that moment of distraction Mrs Pargeter picked up Gary's pink, white and gold china cat and brought it down with all the force of which she was capable on to Derek Bardon's head.

He crumpled and fell in exactly the same way as Edmund Grainger had a little earlier.

Following the precedent set by Kelvin Mitchell, Mrs Pargeter found some bits of clothesline in the kitchen and trussed up her victim hand and foot.

Then, going against the habits of a lifetime, she rang the police to report that she had an intruder in the house.

She looked at Derek Bardon to see if he was still breathing. He was.

And then she looked, with satisfaction, at the smashed shards of pink, white and gold china that lay around his limp body.

THIRTY

'I could replace it,' said Gary as he drove the Bentley sedately towards Girdstone Manor. 'Buy you another one. Because I know how much you liked it.'

Oh dear, thought Mrs Pargeter. Her polite thanks for the china cat had been interpreted as enthusiasm. She would have to find a diplomatic way out of her current social dilemma. 'I think the trouble is, Gary,' she began cautiously, 'that because of the circumstances in which the cat was broken – you know, with me being attacked by that monster – it's always going to have unhappy associations for me. So I think if you were to give me a replacement, it'd just, I don't know . . . well, it'd bring it all back.'

'No, I fully understand that,' said Gary. Hooray, she'd got away with it. But he went on, 'It'd be better if I bought you something completely different.'

Mrs Pargeter winced. She wondered what new artefact Gary's dodgy taste would soon be inflicting on her.

She tried further diversionary tactics. 'You don't have to buy me anything, Gary. Just having you in my life is all that I need.'

The chauffeur glowed, reading rather more into her words than had been intended. But, of course, Mrs Pargeter was unaware of that.

The bride and groom looked stunning. Sammy's dark hair was lustrous above her white dress, contrasting perfectly with Kelvin's ash blond and black suit.

All her friends from the hen party, including Erin Jarvis, had dressed up spectacularly, and Girdstone Manor did prove to be the ideal venue for the occasion. The guests' every desire seemed to be anticipated.

The one thing that did strike a discordant note with Truffler and Gary was that Kelvin Mitchell, through his cousins in the constabulary, had organized a guard of honour of uniformed policemen, who led the way into the chapel.

'Still doesn't feel quite comfortable, does it?' said Truffler.

'No,' said Gary.

Once everyone was in the chapel, the Reverend Holy Smirke conducted a beautiful service. He had talked a lot to the young couple, so his remarks about them sounded really personal. From a pew at the back, his 'housekeeper' Ernestine watched with pride.

During the service, Mrs Pargeter, dressed in a sumptuous turquoise ensemble with cartwheel hat, looked along the rows with pride. Gizmo Gilbert was there, wearing an ostentatiously new suit. Mrs Pargeter had introduced him to a young entrepreneur who was keen to develop 'The Zipper Zapper' commercially, so it looked as though Gizmo's money troubles might be over.

And Mrs Pargeter had told him how his invention had been instrumental in saving her life. He was duly gratified.

Sitting a little in front of her was Helena Winthrop with Napper Johnson at her side. Their heads nestled close together. Since meeting Napper, Helena had been transformed. Gradually, the Botox effect of her upbringing had worn off, and her face had relaxed into something almost girlish. Napper was just as ecstatic as she was.

Mrs Pargeter had already arranged with Sammy that Helena should be the one targeted to catch the bouquet. It wouldn't be long before all memories of her unhappy marriage to Sir Normington Winthrop (or Hair-Trigger Hardcastle) would be washed away by a new, happy marriage.

Mrs Pargeter felt a warm glow. Though she could never recapture the fulfilment she had felt while her husband was alive, she was more than happy with her new family, made up mostly of his former associates.

And as she looked fondly along their ranks, she was unaware of a pair of eyes from the row behind fixed on her throughout the service. But then she never had been aware of Gary's devotion. Nor of the fact that his main preoccupation at that moment was thinking of a suitable replacement for her china cat.